LIGHTS, CAMERA, *Knot*

KAY LYNN

Published by Kayla Grosse writing as Kay Lynn

Printed in the United States of America

First US Edition: April 2026

ISBN: 979-8-9923007-4-1

E-book ASIN: B0FG6ZBWBZ

Cover Design: Brenna Jones

Cover Art: Fremuard

Edited by: Kay Morton

To all my hyper-independent, overworked babes who secretly
dream of being fated to a pack of dangerously hot males who
give you multiple orgasms and take care of you...
this one's for us.

Author's Note

Dear Spicy Reader,

Welcome to the Angel City Omega universe. This is the first book in the series, and you're in for a fun ride! It's very high-heat, so if you're not a fan of spice...you probably don't want to read this book. If you are...YAY! You're in the right place.

Below you'll find the contents/tropes in this book, if you want to be surprised flip to the next page. If you'd like to know what you're in for, keep reading!

- Unexpected heat

- Touch starvation

- Long-term use of heat suppressants

- Scent matches

- MMFMM (two of the M's are together)

- Double penetration

- Double vaginal penetration

- Anal

- Fisting

- Oral

- Mouth knotting

- Mating bonds/bites

- Derogatory language

- Spanking

- Alpha going into rut

- Dominant Alphas

- Messy, cum-filled heat

- Talk of breeding/having children (no pregnancy)

If you'd like more information on this book or any of my books, please visit https://www.kaylagrosse.com.

Now, who's ready to meet Iris and Pack Quinn?

Xoxo,

Kayla

The Pack Quinn Cocktail

Ingredients:

- 2 oz gin (best for carrying herbs) *or vodka*

- 1 oz fresh strawberry purée

- ¾ oz fresh lemon juice

- ¾ oz honey syrup *(1:1 honey + warm water)*

- 4 fresh mint leaves

- 3 fresh basil leaves

- Ice

Strawberry Purée:

Blend 1 cup fresh strawberries and 1 tsp sugar. Strain if you want it silky.

Instructions:

In a shaker, add mint + basil first and gently press once (don't shred or it turns bitter). Add in gin/vodka, strawberry purée, lemon juice and honey syrup. Fill with ice and shake hard for 12 seconds. Double strain into a rocks glass over fresh ice. (Sub club soda for gin/vodka for a delicious virgin option!)

What is Omegaverse?

Omegaverse reshapes relationships and dynamics through a system of secondary genders, classified as Alphas, Betas, or Omegas, with each role shaping social expectations, biology, and intimacy in unique ways.

Alphas are generally dominant and protective. They carry a physiological trait called a knot—a swelling at the base of their anatomy that can lock them to a partner during sex, often associated with fertility and ensuring pregnancy. Within packs, there's usually a **Prime Alpha**, the most dominant of the group, who naturally takes the lead. Even in packs with multiple Alphas, the Prime Alpha's instincts, authority, and pheromonal strength place them at the top of the hierarchy. Alphas also possess something called an **Alpha bark**, a tone to their voice that commands instinctive obedience or stillness in others, often used to assert control or protect their pack.

Betas are the most neutral designation, closest to "average humans." They don't go through heats or ruts, and while their pheromones exist, they aren't as strong. Betas often act as the steady ground between Alpha intensity and Omega instinct.

Omegas are the counterparts to Alphas and often the center of a pack. They experience heats—periods of fertility and desire—and can produce slick, a natural lubricant that helps during sex and intimacy. Omegas may be seen as softer or more submissive but can also be very strong and resilient. All genders can be Omegas, but male-presenting Omegas cannot get pregnant.

Heats & Ruts: Omegas cycle into heats; Alphas into ruts. Both are periods of overwhelming instinct and desire that can disrupt daily life or deepen bonds depending on how they're handled. Omega's can have "heat spikes" during their pre-heat cycle, which is like a mini-heat that needs to be eased, warning their heat is coming within a week to days.

Heat cycles (estrous) can last three to five days. During this time the Omega will go through waves of heat that need to be eased with knots followed by short periods of rest. They experience a strong instinct to nest, creating a warm, safe, scent-soaked space to rest between waves and regulate their hormones. This goes on until the cycle is complete.

Ruts are shorter, and can last up to twenty-four hours or less, with the Alpha driven by sharp, fast-building urges that push them to seek release in quick, intense intervals until the rut burns itself out. They can be eased by any willing partner, but are quicker to burn out with a scent-matched Omega.

Omegas and Alphas can take heat suppressants and rut blockers, however, they aren't always guaranteed to work. If an Omega goes too long on suppressants, it can cause longer and more potent heat cycles when they finally do enter into estrous, as well as "touch starvation." An Omega's hormones are regulated by touch and sex, without these their body struggles to balance pheromone production, leading to heightened sensitivity, irritability, and an overwhelming craving for physical contact once the suppressants wear off.

Likewise, if an Alpha goes for too long without a rut, they are easier to trigger and the Alpha can become more irritable as time goes on, especially if they are a Prime Alpha.

Pheromones & Scent: Everyone carries a unique scent tied to their emotions and state of being. Scents can attract, comfort, warn, or overwhelm. When two (or more) scents blend perfectly, it's called a scent match, an instinctual recognition of compatibility. Think of it like a soulmate or destiny.

You can also be "scent sensitive" to another Alpha, Omega, or Beta, which means your scents are compatible, but this isn't as strong as a scent match and is more common to find. Most packs/pairings are scent sensitive. Omegas can "perfume" when they're emotionally stirred or aroused, their scent intensifies and fills the space around them, acting like a beacon to their pack. Perfuming can happen at any time, but chances of it are stronger around compatible matches and packmates, and close to/during a heat cycle.

There is also the instinctive act of *scent marking*, where one will transfer their scent onto their partner's skin or clothing. This is a primal way of claiming, comforting, or signaling a bond recognizable to other people/packs.

Pack Bonds: Alphas and Betas can form a pack bond, which is initiated by the Prime Alpha marking the others somewhere on the body (not the neck). This type of bond links everyone on an emotional level. They can sense general feelings, shifts in mood, and the stability of the group. Pack bonds do not require sex, and they can exist without an Omega. They create unity, structure, and hierarchy, allowing a pack to function as a cohesive unit.

Claiming Bonds: This occurs when an Alpha has sex with and knots their chosen partner—usually an Omega—and then bites the neck to seal the bond. Claiming is intensely physical, instinctual, and rare for Betas or Alphas to receive from another Alpha. When an Omega is claimed, and the Omega claims the pack back with a bite (anywhere on the body), the bond creates a mate connection. Emotions become sharper, pheromones synchronize, and the pack can sense each other with more precision. This kind of connection can only be done with an Omega.

Further Notes About the Angel City Omegaverse World:

- **Important:** In this universe, the Omega, Alpha, and Beta aren't just designations, they're instinctual parts of a person. Almost like a second voice under the skin. Characters can feel their designation responding inside them, pushing, warning, or urging them on, which is why they'll say things like "my Alpha" or "my Omega" as if it's someone they can talk to.

- Scents are an important part of designation dynamics, they help identify mood, and potential mates or packmates. Because of that, scents aren't usually blocked completely. In enclosed or professional spaces like film sets, de-scenters are sprayed to dampen scents so they don't get overwhelming. There are products that can block scents entirely, like sprays and deodorants, but they're difficult to maintain and burn off quickly, so most people don't bother. Neutralizer sprays can be used inside the nose to stop someone from smelling scents altogether, though they're mainly used by doctors or others who need to avoid pheromone exposure.

- Omegas can bond at any time, not only in heat, as long as the claiming includes a knot. Without the knot, it's only a simple pack bond, not a true mating bond tied to emotions.

- The first claim should always come from the Prime Alpha on the neck, ensuring the strongest connection for the pack and the Omega.

- Omegas don't have to bond with a pack's Beta, especially if the Beta is already pack-bonded to the Prime Alpha or through a claiming with another Alpha, but they may choose to for deeper intimacy and connection.

- Omegas can only become pregnant during heat. Regular birth-control shots can prevent conception during that time.

- Omegas are built to take knots. Alphas and Betas can take knots, but it requires the right amount of preparation and lubrication for it to be safe and pleasurable.

Chapter One

Iris

"WHAT DO YOU MEAN they can't refill my suppressant prescription?" I shout to my assistant and friend, Sadie, as I pace the length of my Star Trailer, my usual sweet strawberry scent turning bitter.

"They wouldn't let me, Iris. The pharmacist said it wasn't approved by your doctor."

"Oh no," I groan. "You can't be serious."

"I'm sorry. I tried. I even had them call the office but it didn't work."

The voice of my regular doctor last week saying, *"You need to have a normal heat or your body will suffer serious consequences,"* rings through my memory. That's why I went to a new one. A doctor who works at a very sought after "Omega only" clinic in Beverly Hills. My agent assured me that if I went to an appointment there, I wouldn't have a problem getting another round of suppressants prescribed to me. Or at least enough to get me through the next month of shooting this big budget romantic comedy, *Knotting Hill*. The role of a lifetime, one that every actor would kill to have.

"Did they call the new doctor's office or my old one?"

"The one on the prescription."

"Ugh, that's the new one then!" I twirl a lock of my long dark brown hair as I continue to pace. "I don't understand! That doctor assured me they'd fill it."

"I don't know, Iris. I'm so, so sorry. I tried everything, I swear."

A high-pitched whine explodes out of me, my high-heeled feet wearing a hole into the expensive furry white rug I requested in my trailer. It's beautiful and soft. The kind of rug my Omega wants to faceplant in right now before covering herself in a million blankets, transforming the floor into a makeshift nest. But I can't do that. I won't do that. I have a movie to shoot and today is my first day on set. I can't show up out of sorts; I need to get myself together and make a good first impression.

I stop pacing in front of her. "Do you still have the prescription?"

She shakes her head, her short black bob with peekaboo blue highlights brushing her round cheeks. "No, they took it from me."

I blow out a breath as I observe her. Sadie's a sweet Beta who's been my assistant and a good friend for a couple years now, and by the wide-eyed look on her face combined with her smell, I've terrified her. Her light lavender scent that often calms me reeks of dying flowers. My stomach flips and nausea bubbles up my throat.

"I'm sorry for yelling, I know it's not your fault. I'm just stressed," I say.

More than stressed. But I shouldn't take it out on Sadie. If I should be upset at anyone it's my agent and the doctor. I'm *really* pissed at him. Why did he deny my prescription when he wrote the damn thing in the first place? *Fucking, fuck!*

"Is there anything I can do to help?" Sadie asks. "I was told there's an entire department with nesting supplies. I could go and get some items for you if that would comfort you—"

"No!" My Omega tries to protest again but I cut her off. She may want nesting supplies our nice Beta friend offered to get us, but I'm not going to cave. Not only because I don't want to hide and get all out of sorts then have to force myself out of comfort to go on set and work, but I don't need to throw myself into a heat faster. Nesting would for sure put my hormones out of whack more than they already are. And if the supplies are from old movie and TV sets, the smells will be all over the place and that won't do.

"Okay." Sadie reaches out to place her hand on my shoulder. She squeezes it gently. "You remember that my sisters are Omegas, right?"

I nod. "Of course."

"My mom used to make this natural tea to help curb pre-heat symptoms. I'll see if I can get that. Are you feeling anything that would make you think your heat is coming soon?"

I close my eyes and tap into my instincts. My Omega has been high-strung lately because I've been on suppressants for too long without a break. She wants to go home to our condo, sit in her comfy nest with the twinkly lights on the ceiling above, and eat Rocky Road ice cream, maybe use our battery-operated friend with a silicone knot to ease the ache I've been ignoring between my thighs for months now.

However, none of those things are pre-heat symptoms, they're natural Omega responses to stress and to being on suppressants long term. I shouldn't be showing any pre-heat signs yet. I only took my last dose yesterday, and since I've been on them for a full year, it should take some time for them to clear my system.

The last time I came off, I'd been using them for six months and it took two weeks before symptoms like a low-grade fever appeared, and I had my first heat spike that I eased with said silicone knot. Logically, after a year, it should take longer...maybe a month. That's what I'm hoping for. Then again, last time I was isolated on vacation, with hardly any scents around me, no hot Alphas in sight, and none of the stress of work pressing down on me.

I swallow hard and squeeze my eyes shut. No, no. I can't stress myself out more than I already am or think of sexy Alphas. I have to think positively.

It *will* take me longer to have pre-heat symptoms. I *will* be fine. I can get through this month-long shoot without incident. I *need to* make it through. There's no other choice. This is my absolute dream role and I'm lucky to even be here considering I'm a replacement. The last Omega, Molly, an actor whose star has been on the rise the last year, had to pull out because she found out she was pregnant and was having horrible morning sickness that lasted most of the day.

When my agent called and said the role was mine if I wanted it, I said yes without a second thought. Had I planned to take time off to safely go off suppressants, have my heat at a clinic with a scent-sensitive pack instead of alone, and then get a new prescription filled? Yes. But like I said, my agent assured me I could get it refilled with her fancy Hollywood doctor.

"Iris?"

I take another large inhale and exhale before I open my eyes to Sadie's worried green ones. I've been standing here with my eyes clamped shut and a death grip on the lock of hair I'd been twirling.

I drop my hair, scalp tingling, and hold my hands in front of me. "I'm not having any symptoms. At least not yet."

My Omega tries to object but once again I shut her down.

Gods, what's wrong with her? It's got to be the stress that's triggering this overreaction. Not having my suppressants is bad but I shouldn't be whining at the idea of not having symptoms. Especially since I did take that last suppressant yesterday.

We're fine, I assure her and myself. Another godforsaken whine rises in my throat and I swallow it. *Fuck*! Like I said, my Omega has been high-strung, but in general she's always been sensitive; it's part of what makes me a great actor. But I'm not going to let anything ruin this for me, especially my biology.

We can make it through this, and then I'll let her—and let's be honest, me—have what we want. Time off. Touch. Big fat knots ruining us. Maybe instead of a run-of-the-mill heat clinic, I'll splurge and go to the fancy one in Malibu other Omega actors rave about with very experienced and attractive Alphas. I'm getting a nice paycheck from this gig so I could afford it. I heard they even have different themed nests with the best sheets money can buy.

"Do you want me to get the tea anyway?" Sadie asks.

I blink and clear my throat. My little train of thought there was very, very bad. Another second thinking about knots and nests, and I would have been perfuming, or worse yet, making a mess of my underwear with slick. Hair and makeup have already taken care of me, so I wouldn't have been able to shower, and the last thing I need is to be smelling like ripe and ready to pick strawberry fields in front of everyone on set. Including my very attractive Alpha costar, Jett Quinn, who the entire world has a crush on, me included.

"Yes, please," I answer Sadie. I may not be in pre-heat but maybe the tea will calm my Omega. "And no matter how much I ask for sweets, don't get me any," I say just before I request ice cream. "Also, no caffeine. Those two things can bring on a heat faster." Caffeine already isn't great for an Omega's sensitive system, adding it in plus the comfort of sugar would be not good.

"Do you want me to get you anything else?"

I wrack my brain for other ideas that could keep my system calm and ensure I make it through this shoot without incident.

"Oh! Get some of that extra strength de-scenting spray and deodorant. I'll spray my clothes and layer it over my scent glands."

"Okay."

I snap my fingers. "Oh! And that neutralizer spray, the kind you can shoot up your nose."

Sadie scrunches her nose at the same time I do. That stuff is disgusting. Doctors use it because their jobs involve saving lives, they can't risk their biology taking over when someone good-smelling walks in. I don't know any actors who use it. I never have. But I've also never completely blocked my scent with sprays and deodorants before, either. It's not a common thing to do.

"I know it's gross, but I think it's for the best. If my Omega even thinks one of those Alphas or Betas on set smells good, it could bring on my heat faster. That's the last thing I need."

Sadie agrees and makes notes on her phone before looking back up at me, her brow furrowed. "You said you just took your last suppressant yesterday, right?"

"Yeah, but as you probably know with your Omega sisters, if someone is scent-sympathetic or gods forbid scent-matched with my Omega, I could perfume or worse yet, have a heat spike. Without the suppressant in my system daily, there will be nothing to stop that from happening. And if that happens, I'm screwed. They would kick me off the set so none of the Alphas go into rut and I'd lose my job, more jobs in the future too."

She nods. "I understand. There's a store down the road. I can get everything now and be back before you go on set."

I give her a genuine smile, a bit calmer now that I have a plan, even if my Omega thinks said plan is dumb. Especially hiding my ability to smell and my scent from potential matches or even a rare scent match. Finding your scent-matched mate or mates is an Omega's dream come true, but that's not going to happen. Not only is it rare, but I don't have time to pack up and settle down. I have my future career to think about. A career where I'm more than just the curvy Omega that was on the hit young adult vampire show *Knot Hollows*. Instead, I'm a respected film actor. One that wins Oscars.

My Omega protests in frustration at my choices, but this is how it has to be. Not only for my career, but for everyone's safety. When I got this job I assured production I was on suppressants. Biology can be a bitch, and an Omega going into heat, even pre-heat, on set with Alphas present is a liability. Alphas are also required to provide proof they're on rut blockers. Unfortunately, even with that it's dangerous for an unbonded Omega to be in an enclosed space with them if said Omega isn't on suppressants or anywhere close to heat.

Gods, maybe this idea is stupid. But when I think of leaving set, of giving up this opportunity of a lifetime, it physically pains me.

No, I can do this. I can deny my biological instincts. It will be okay.

"Are you sure you're good?"

"Yes, thanks for doing all this, Sadie. And sorry again for yelling at you."

"It's okay. I know how important this job is to you and I can't imagine how stressful this must be."

I wring my hands and look around at the trailer. It's the nicest one I've been in, spacious, stocked full of food and drinks. It's fit for the lead of a big-budget romantic comedy. Which is what I am.

"This could be it, Sadie. This role could change everything."

While I'm best known for playing a vampire named Genevive on *Knot Hollows* in my twenties, I've had other roles since the show went off the air five years ago. Unfortunately, I've been pigeonholed so most of them are similar gigs or small character spots on TV. I make a decent living but I've always wanted to be more. To make my way into film and be taken seriously by all my peers.

This part of Juliette in *Knotting Hill* could do that. Plus, alongside starring opposite of Jett, I'm going to work with the leading studio in the business, Genesis Studios. They're producing the best content out there right now, and Pack Quinn who own and operate it, are Jett's pack. From the knowledge I have of them, they all met in film school and bonded into a pack, then created their studio.

A pack without an Omega...

I brush that thought off and tell my Omega to behave. The fact they don't have an Omega yet doesn't matter and has nothing to do with why I want to work with them so badly. Not only does the three-Alpha-and-one-Beta pack produce quality content, they're also progressive thinkers that make thought provoking shows, featuring people of all body types in their work. Body types like my plus-size one. Which isn't the norm for an Omega. Most of my designation is short, thin, and lightly curved in all the right places. I'm tall, heavy breasted, and big hipped. I literally have meat on every inch of me. Not that I mind. At least not anymore. I'm confident in who I am, and that's that.

Sadie slides her phone in her jean pocket before holding out her arms for a hug. I step into them easily and exhale a breath, letting her hold me. She's been such a great assistant and companion for the last three years. With my schedule, I hardly have time to breathe let alone get a friend group. Then there's dating. No time for that either. If I need a hug, Sadie provides.

I breathe in her lavender scent that's back to normal now, and allow myself to melt into her embrace and soothe some of my stress. The way I'm at ease with even a platonic Beta hug is a stark reminder of what my doctor told me last week.

One of the biggest reasons he said I needed to go off my suppressants and have a heat was that my blood panels showed abnormal cortisol levels indicating touch starvation and undue stress to my body. I tried to deny it, but with how my Omega's been lately, I knew he was right. The oversensitivity, wanting ice cream, the ache between my thighs...

My system is out of whack and I need to have a heat with Alphas. Not only that, I need to feel strong hands on my body and a knot stretching my pussy, or more than one knot. It's been far too long. Unfortunately, it will need to be a bit longer.

I hug Sadie tighter before pulling back. "Thanks."

"You're welcome. I'll get everything and be back soon. You stay and run your lines. They shouldn't need you for another hour."

We say our goodbyes and I lock the door behind her. I walk to the small dining table in the trailer, picking up my script and looking down at the cover page. *Knotting Hill* by August Quinn.

My stomach flips thinking of the hunky Beta who reminds me of Clark Kent but with lighter brown hair and thick-framed glasses. He's an amazing writer and a two-time Oscar winner. I've been watching his work for years now and have dreamed of getting to bring one of his layered characters to life. I can't wait to meet him. Not only him but his whole pack.

The only pack member I've spoken to is their lead Alpha, Wilder, who's the director of the film. My toes curl when I think of his deep and soothing voice during our phone chat prior to my arrival. It reminded me of a calming cup of mint tea. It made me wonder if he smelled like it too. I shake that thought from my head. The entire pack is attractive, and I'm going to just have to deal with it. It's not like I haven't worked with attractive men before. This town is full of them.

I move to the couch and sit with the script in my lap. This really could be the beginning of something bigger for me. I know it. I'm going to have to be strong and keep my focus. No matter if Wilder's voice makes my toes curl, or August looks like a hotter Clark Kent, or if Jett's beautiful blue eyes captivate me more than any Alpha's ever have even through a screen. There's also the third Alpha, Mateo, the cinematographer, who's layered black hair and dark brown eyes would make anyone's underwear melt.

"No." I clear my throat. "It doesn't matter at all."

Yep, everything is going to be just fine.

Chapter Two

August

"Our Beta looks like he's going to hurl his guts up."

I narrow my green eyes at my Prime, but Wilder's right. I do feel like I'm going to hurl. I take a shallow breath through my mouth. "I'm fine."

"He's nervous about meeting Iris finally. You know he's been crushing on her since before we all met in college, right?" my Alpha packmate and mate, Mateo, asks rhetorically as he adjusts a light on the bookstore set while other production assistants, grips, and sound artists mill around us, getting ready for our first day of shooting with our new Omega lead.

The handsome asshole knows Wilder already has this information. My whole pack knows it. It only became more of a topic since Iris's audition for *Knotting Hill* came to us last fall and I practically begged Wilder and Jett to cast her until the film's investors convinced us to go with "rising Omega star Molly" before she got pregnant.

"Sometimes I think he loves *Knot Hollows* more than he loves me and our pack," Mateo adds.

Wilder snorts and I turn to him. He smirks from the director's chair seated next to mine, rubbing a tattooed hand over his well-trimmed beard as he glances from Mateo to me, wiggling his eyebrows in a way that seems too playful for how huge and intimidating the Alpha is with his dark tresses in an undercut pompadour-style haircut and all his ink.

I look back to Mateo. "You know that's not true. And you like watching too sometimes, in case you forgot."

"It's a good show and Iris was phenomenal in it, but you still binge it, mi amor."

My heart flutters at the endearment he's called me since the early days of our relationship, even before he gave me his claiming bite on my neck and bonded me for life our junior year of college. But that's not going to make me less annoyed at him for outing me in front of everyone who's not my pack in ear shot. At least Iris isn't on set now. We haven't met yet, and the last thing I want is for her to hear I'm a major fanboy before we even have a chance to shake hands.

I grunt, cheeks turning pink. "Haven't you heard of comfort shows, Mateo?" It's the only thing I can think of to say right now.

Wilder is silent but I sense him eyeing me and the pack bond I have with him buzzing at attention, making sure I don't become too upset by the teasing. I may not be in an intimate relationship with him or my other packmate, Jett, beyond helping them through ruts on a rare occasion, but I love them. And as our Prime—the leader and most dominant of our pack—he's always watching and directing. It's what makes him so good at his job, too. He's level-headed, fair, yet strong. Everything a good Prime should be.

Mateo finishes his light set up and nods at a Beta helping him before he prowls over, his honey scent wafting into my nose. He places his hands on the arms of the chair, encroaching his six-foot-two muscular body into my space, his earthy brown eyes alight with mischief and pink lips that look way too kissable in an apologetic half-grin.

"I'm sorry if I embarrassed you, mi amor," he says so only Wilder and I can hear. "I was just trying to lighten you up a bit since Iris will be here soon."

I stare into his eyes, feeling the sincerity and apology of his words through his tone and our bond. I exhale and dip my chin in acceptance. "It's fine. Just don't do it in front of Iris, please."

"I won't," he assures me.

Wilder pats my back. "If he does, I'll kick him off set for you."

Mateo balks and stands, crossing his arms over his T-shirt clad chest. "You can't kick me out, then who would do your lights, compa?"

"Your crew."

He mutters curses in Spanish before stepping in front of Wilder. "They're good, but they need me and you know it."

Wilder and Mateo bicker like an old married couple, their chests puffing out as they do their Alpha posturing or whatever. There was a time when I was younger that I wished I'd designate as an Alpha, but I'm very happy being a Beta. I like not having to worry about ruts or being the biggest, most dominant in the room. I'm perfectly happy writing screenplays, being the calming balm to my Alphas, and giving Mateo the love he deserves. Maybe someday we'll have an Omega too, but with Jett's fame and our pack's studio getting busier, that seems less likely every year.

The attention we get from Omega's now tends to be from those that want to use us for fame or money, and not because they want to be a member of our pack. There's also something else. From the outside looking in, you'd never think my manly Alphas are romantics, especially with the playboy rep the pack tends to get due to our openness when it comes to sex outside of the pack, but they are. They dream of finding our scent match, even if that's rare.

I won't lie and say I haven't dreamt about it too, especially since Mateo and I are as close to a scent match as a Beta and Alpha can be and we'd love to start a family one day. I knew he was mine the moment our honey and basil scents twined together that day he sat next to me in Film 101 our first day of college. Finding Wilder with his sharp yet soothing mint and Jett with his tart lemon later that year only made our pack complete. Well, almost complete. We're just missing something...

Or should I say someone.

"You know you could never function without me," Mateo scoffs. "Tell him, mi amor."

"You know you couldn't, Wilder," I say, meeting the large Alpha's gaze.

He opens his mouth, most likely to joke that everyone is replaceable, even though we all know that's not true. Mateo is the best cinematographer in the game right now. Moreover, Wilder would shit if anyone else tried to light our films. The two of them just like to push each other's buttons like brothers would, but it's always in good fun. The worst that's ever come of it is one not talking to the other for a few hours, but then they always make up and life goes on.

"I know this was already approved, but do you like this shirt?" Jett walks up, interrupting the conversation before Wilder can speak. "Or will it wash me out?"

The three of us turn to look at our missing packmate who's standing next to Mateo now. The white linen button up is partially open as his deft fingers work each small button into its slot, slowly covering up some of his scattered tattoos, and six pack dusted in dark blond chest hair. His blue eyes meet ours as he finishes the last button, sliding his hands over the sleeves to smooth them out.

"Did you just ask me that question?" Wilder chuffs.

"Are you lighting?" Jett volleys.

Mateo snickers and slings his arm over Jett's broad shoulders, grinning smugly at Wilder with a clear message playing on his features: *See, you need me.*

Our Prime just shakes his head and Mateo grins wider, pulling back from Jett so he can see his full outfit.

"It doesn't wash you out. Especially with that gold California tan you've got going on."

Jett cringes. "Fuck, did I screw up? I didn't mean to stay out in the sun that long this weekend, but I took advantage of the last days off."

We know he did. The man was gone for the entire weekend, to the point any of us hardly saw him. I thought maybe he was sowing his wild oats but I guess he was surfing. He's not originally from California, but you'd never know. He's a southern boy from the landlocked state of Kentucky, which I think is why he likes the ocean so much and picked up surfing during college. If he's not acting or finding a female or females to spend the night with—or ones to share with Wilder—he's at the beach or the gym.

Mateo's gaze flicks over him again with a critical eye. "Hmm, it doesn't wash you out, but..." He trails off, and I watch as his brain works. His dark brow furrows and his pupils track back and forth as he thinks. I'm not going to lie, it's a turn on.

I love smart men, and Mateo's not only smart but incredibly creative and an artist of light. He's been taking photographs and honing his skills since he was a child. He's won multiple awards, including several Mexican-American Film and Television Festival & Awards and his first Oscar win last year. Like I said, he's incredible. And mine.

Wilder knocks my shoulder and leans over so only I can hear him. "Don't make the set smell like an Italian restaurant."

I shift in my chair, cheeks turning pink with a new type of embarrassment. I wouldn't make the whole set smell like basil since Beta's pheromones aren't as strong as Alpha's or Omega's, but with our pack bond and awareness of each other's scents, it's not a surprise that Wilder smelled my little spike of arousal. Normally I'm able to control myself but I think my nerves over meeting Iris and the first day of shooting have let it slip a little.

I clear my throat. "Sorry."

Wilder quietly laughs as Mateo steps next to my chair so he can get a better look at Jett. He leans over, his lips brushing against my ear. "Later, mi amor."

My damn basil scent spikes again and I bite back a groan, hiding my slight hard-on with my laptop. *Fucking Alphas.*

"But?" Jett asks.

"Actually"—Mateo walks around him and studies the bookstore set beyond before stepping back in front of him—"I think it's fine. We haven't shot anything with you yet so we won't need to worry about color correction there. But you realize you're going to have to keep this tan through the shoot for continuity."

He nods. "That shouldn't be a problem as long as Wilder lets me out of the studio and into the sunlight."

Wilder grips his laptop, the corner of his lip lifting. "It's not my fault we're on a time crunch, but you'll still have breaks to go bake in the sun. If worse comes to worse, I can have a PA rent a tanning bed for you, princess."

Jett growls and we all hold back laughter. He hates when we call him a princess. He really isn't one when it comes down to it; the man was raised on a farm, but with everything he does to maintain his Most Eligible Alpha status, including a very careful, haircare, skincare, and diet/gym regime, not to mention his closet of designer clothes, it's an easy way to tease him. Even if everything he does is a necessary part of his job as an actor.

"There's also this thing called self-tanner," Mateo says, tucking a bit of his textured nearly-black hair behind his ear. "Just make sure makeup is aware."

Jett's growl ceases but he still maintains an annoyed look on his diamond-shaped face with the perfect amount of dark blond beard that's been freshly trimmed. "The real sun will be just fine, but hair and makeup will be made aware regardless."

"Now that that's settled," Wilder says, motioning Jett with two fingers to look at something on his laptop screen. "I was talking to Augie about a small change to the dialogue of this first scene where your character Hugh meets Juliette at her bookstore."

Jett's gaze flicks from the screen to me. "Have you had a PA send the new pages out?"

I shake my head. "It was something recent that I wanted to run by you first." The movie we're shooting is a romcom inspired by a trip we took to a seaside town last year. I had a dream about a beautiful voluptuous Omega who's a bookshop owner in the sleepy ocean town of Knotting Hill. Her world is turned upside down when a famous Alpha actor unexpectedly walks into her store and their unlikely romance ensues.

This role is natural for Jett, and I'm not going to lie and say I wasn't picturing Iris as the bookshop owner from the start. Molly is an amazing actor, and she was going to be a great Juliette and bring great press to our film due to her rising star after the last hit movie she was in, but she wasn't the one I really wanted.

When she ended up pregnant, I was ecstatic. Not because she was sick, that was terrible, but because I knew she was happy about the unexpected baby and so was her new pack. It also meant we got to put in the call to have Iris replace her. When I found out she could accept on short notice, I was so excited I nearly passed out. Not that I'd tell any of my pack that, even if Mateo probably knew from the way I was practically vibrating.

Jett studies the line with the change, then looks up to me and Wilder. "That's fine, I can remember that no problem. Looks like you didn't change Iris's so no need to send out the pages, you can just make her aware when she gets here."

"Must be nice to have a photographic memory," I tease.

"It's a perk." He grins, the charming smile that's helped make him famous sparking across his features. If Jett and I had a sexual relationship beyond helping with ruts if needed, I'd be smelling like crushed basil right now. Honestly, I don't know how actors work with him, especially Omegas. I'd go into heat the moment I got a whiff of his lemon scent, or at the very least perfume every time we did a scene together.

There were times, especially at the beginning of his career, that he tried to have relationships with his costars, but after a stalking incident that ended with a restraining order, Jett makes it clear that he won't fuck his costars. Their relationships are to be professional only. He's held true to that for years now. By proxy, our pack doesn't sleep with anyone we work with either.

"I think we're ready to call her in," Wilder says as he looks over the set. "You're good, Mateo?"

"Yep, all good."

"Great. We can run through blocking and lines when she gets here, then we can shoot the first scene. If we stay on track the first few days we should be able to finish in the next four weeks as planned."

"You're speaking like a naive director fresh out of film school." Mateo laughs.

"I'm trying to be optimistic," he grouses. "If we go over we risk ruining our future production schedules for the rest of the year. And we'd lose money."

Between all of us and a trust fund my parents left me when they passed away a few years ago, my pack isn't hurting for money. But our Prime is a perfectionist and likes things to run like a well-oiled machine. And I get what he's saying. It's not like my trust fund could produce every film we do, and it would be bad to anger our investors and risk future productions, including relationships with crew and actors.

I grip Wilder's arm, right over the black-and-grey ouroboros inked into his bicep, the same tattoo all of us wear on our right arm. I push out a wave of steady Beta calm through our bond, letting it settle over my pack, all of us still on edge from the reminder that even though I'm glad Iris is here, Molly's exit right before production threw everything off.

We were supposed to start shooting a week ago but we were able to push a week to sign contracts and give Iris a bit of time to learn her lines and get fitted with wardrobe. Thankfully her and Molly are similar in size, though Iris is a bit curvier and taller than she is.

"It will be fine," I assure them. "We've shot on tight schedules before," I remind them. "Remember the *Knot Good News* production?"

Everyone groans. That was one of our first big films as a studio where we got outside funding. It was a dramatic heist-style movie. It was nightmare after nightmare. The cast of Alphas and Betas we chose to star with Jett ended up being complete assholes who partied every night and showed up hungover. There were several points during that shoot where we almost gave up on our dream of Genesis Studios being successful, but we pulled through and that film put us on the map.

"How could I forget?" Jett growls. "I still dream of punching half of those actor's lights out."

"Same," Wilder grunts. "But, Augie is right. We've gotten through worse, and from everything I've heard of Iris, she's a professional and great to work with. Everything will be smooth sailing."

I dip my chin and smile at my pack. "It will be, I know it."

Wilder smiles back. "I'll get a PA to bring her to the set."

CHAPTER THREE

Iris

I'VE BEEN ON FILM sets for most of my adult life, but walking on to a soundstage will never get old. The people, the lights, the sounds, I love it. I usually even like the odd mixture of scents because they tell stories of those who filmed there before me.

Right now, though, I don't smell anything except "hospital" due to the sterile neutralizer I sprayed up my nostrils. It's disgusting, truly, and if I hadn't shoved my Omega far down and drank an entire pot of pre-heat tea before I got called on set, I know she'd be whining and pushing me to go to the bathroom to blow my nose and wash off all the different de-scenting agents I layered over my scent glands and under my armpits. I hope Jett doesn't cringe when he meets me, not that I would blame him. I'd cringe if I smelled me, but this is the only option I have right now, so I'll have to pretend like it's normal.

"Do you want to do a secret signal if you need more neutralizer or I have to make an excuse to get you off set?" Sadie asks quietly from beside me as we follow a PA through another door of the soundstage to where Juliette's bookshop set is.

I shake my head. "I think I'll be fine. It says it lasts a few hours so I should be good till lunch." I want to say if she needs to find a way to get me off set we're going to have way bigger problems. But like I said earlier, I have no pre-heat symptoms and despite the horrible smell in my nose and the nerves of a new job, I'm feeling better. My Omega is quiet, my strawberry scent is locked down, and I won't be able to smell even a hint of any Alpha or

Beta scents. I can't even smell Sadie's and she's right next to me nor wearing any sort of de-scenter.

"Okay, if you're sure."

I squeeze her hand. "Thanks for being here with me."

"Of course, not only is it my job but I'll admit I'm excited too. This is so much different than your usual jobs. Already there's a bunch more people and the energy is buzzing."

She's right. The soundstage is bigger, the equipment is nicer, and with that they have more people working for the film. *Knot Hollows* was a popular and long-running TV show but it didn't have the biggest budget and our A-list guest stars were few and far between.

"You're a Jett fan too, right?" I ask.

Sadie blushes. "Like most people."

"That's true." I laugh. "Sorry I didn't ask sooner."

"You've been busy with everything, and it's not like it really matters anyway."

Busy is a nice word for frazzled. I've been so in my head about the suppressants and learning lines I didn't even think about the fact she gets to be on set with me and meet famous actors like Jett and the others hired for the supporting cast.

"Let's hope he's as nice as people have said," I say. Normally I'd know more about my leading man beyond what I've learned from the media and through the grapevine of other actors I know. We would have had a chemistry test and done a table read, but nothing about this job has been normal so far. Ever since I was offered the role it's been a whirlwind of contracts, doctor's appointments for my failed suppressants, line learning, and wardrobe fittings.

We approach the outer facade of a fake wall that I'm assuming is the bookstore. The PA in front of us slows and steps to the side so we stop with her. "Pack Quinn is right through this door, Ms. Walker," she says. "I'll come and collect you when they call lunch to show you where the main meals will be served. Craft

Services is on the other side of the soundstage if you or your assistant need anything."

"Thank you, um—"

"Maria."

"Thanks, Maria."

"Of course."

I gesture to Sadie. "Do you have a place where Sadie can stay while we shoot?"

"We do." She smiles warmly at my assistant. "You could go to Video Village just over there to watch the live feed of the cameras." Maria points to where there's a couple people, cameras, and an empty director's chair that reads *Wilder Quinn,* along with another one that reads *August Quinn* printed on the fabric.

"Or I can take you back to Iris's trailer," she finishes.

Sadie looks at me and I nod, knowing she's staying like we discussed.

"Video Village, please," Sadie says.

"Of course, you can head that way and take a seat, I'll let the crew know who you are. Iris, you can go on in."

Sadie hugs me and I promise to let her meet Jett and the rest of Pack Quinn later, though she'll be sitting right next to two of them in Video Village. Hopefully she won't combust like I probably would if I was in her shoes. I'm already going to be trying not to combust and I have to work with them and act normally, harder given I no longer have suppressants to take.

Nope. No. Not going there.

"Sounds good. Now go break a leg," Sadie whispers.

I squeeze her a final time before I pull back. After she and the PA have departed I put my hand on the fake door that will lead onto the set. I could probably walk around to the open front but this is where the PA brought me so I guess this is where I'll enter.

I take a large inhale through my nose and immediately decide that was a bad idea because the neutralizer stings my eyes. I fist my hands and blink a few times so they don't water. I don't want to look like I'm crying or ruin my makeup. I gently inhale through my mouth when I'm sure my eyes are clear and mutter, "You can do this, Iris."

"I have no doubt about that."

I jump with a gasp at the male voice behind me and whir around, a hand clutching my chest. My gaze collides with amused brown eyes—though brown doesn't quite cover it. They're the shade of worn leather, soft and supple, with the depth of dark earth or rich burnt mahogany.

The tall, muscular man, who screams Alpha even without scenting him, grins at me. His stance is casual with his hands in the pockets of his jeans like he didn't just scare the absolute crap out of me. I observe him further, his black hair that tapers to the base of his neck, his light amber skin tone and playful aura. When my brain computes this is Mateo Quinn, I inhale through my nose without thinking. I scrunch it again from the sterile smell that makes my nose tingle and my eyes sting once more.

"Easy conejita, I didn't mean to scare you."

I'm not fluent in Spanish, but I understand enough—thanks to living in L.A. since I was eighteen and killing time on set with one of those language apps—to know he just called me little rabbit. Makes sense given my sky-high jump and current look on my face.

Gods, I'm already making a great first impression. Freaking neutralizing spray. I'm going to have to get better about breathing slowly and through my mouth when I can help it. Though that won't be possible while filming. All I can hope is I get used to the smell and slight burn soon.

"It's okay," I assure him. "I thought you were already on set and didn't know someone was behind me."

Mateo holds up a coffee in a paper cup. "Getting a bit of go-go juice before we get started."

I bite my lip to keep from laughing and he smiles, showing off a bit of his straight white teeth. My stomach flips and despite the horrid smell in my nose I'm glad I can't scent him. He's even bigger and sexier than his pictures make him out to be and I don't need any reason for my Omega to get riled up when I just calmed her down.

He closes his lips, mouth still tilted in a sly grin that makes my breath hitch in my chest. I should say something, anything, but no words come. It's annoying since I'm usually good with people and light conversation. I've had to be as an actor, not to mention all my media training I've had helps too. But for some reason, looking into his mahogany eyes, I'm entranced. My stomach flips faster when his gaze flicks down my body, and he runs his tongue over his teeth like he likes what he sees.

Ditto, Alpha.

Alpha...

The pressure of a whine builds in my throat and I'm so shocked by the sudden appearance of my Omega I nearly choke. I quickly put my hand over my mouth and cover it up with a cough while I internally try not to panic at that little mishap.

"Are you okay?" Mateo asks worriedly.

My cheeks flush with embarrassment as I cough a few more times. There should be absolutely no reason to have that kind of reaction to him.

I cough again and meet his concerned gaze. I force a smile on my face and shake my head. "Sorry. Tickle in my throat."

He raises a brow and offers his cup of coffee to me in a sweet gesture.

"It's alright." I swallow. "I don't drink caffeine."

"Ah, right. Sorry, my mate is always asking for coffee. I forget that Omega's don't drink it unless it's decaf."

My brain short circuits hearing him say mate and Omega in the same sentence and for a moment a spark of jealousy slips through from my inner demon—yes, demon. She deserves to be called that with the way she's acting today.

I quietly remind her that I knew this information. It's widely known around town that Mateo and August are together. The Alpha's claiming mark is on the Beta's neck for everyone to see, and I've read the interviews about how they met and soon after found Jett and Wilder to form their pack. It's not unusual for packs to take on a Beta and for them to be bonded into the pack, but it's rarer for an Alpha to be mated to a Beta. It likely means their scent sympathetic and feel connected in a similar way an Alpha would to an Omega—like their souls are better together than apart.

However, all of that doesn't mean the pack isn't looking for an Omega. As far as I know August isn't mated to Jett and Wilder, only pack bonded, and they're open to the idea of having an Omega if the right one comes along. Or at least, that's what all the entertainment sources have said when they talk about the Quinn pack, specifically Jett. Not that it matters. I shouldn't even be thinking about this.

But he's—

"I'm Iris by the way," I cut off my Omega. If she refuses to stay down then I'm going to have to learn to ignore her just like the sterile smell in my nose. Hopefully this will distract him too from that awkward coughing situation and whatever the hell is going on in my body.

Mateo's brow unfurrows and amusement returns into his eyes. He holds out his hand and like an idiot I take it. His warm fingers wrap around my hand, dwarfing it. That's a feat in itself; since I'm tall I don't have dainty hands like a lot of Omegas, or even Betas. Yet his...his hand takes over mine like a flame engulfing tinder, setting me ablaze.

"I know who you are, conejita."

My nose scrunches automatically at the nickname and he squeezes my hand as he shakes it. When I don't answer he continues, "I'm Mateo, but you already knew that, too."

I nod, dumbly, heat licking up my arm and threatening to boil me alive. I pull my hand back abruptly when my throat tightens on another freaking whine, and put it behind my back with the other one, holding them together so I don't do something dumb like reach out and pull his delicious body against me.

"Yes," I fumble out. "It's nice to meet you."

"You too."

We stand in front of the fake set door, our bodies probably too close for people who just met. We may no longer be touching, but I still feel as if I'm on fire, heat and flame crackling between us. It's unlike anything I've ever felt before, and the fact it's happening without us even being able to scent each other is very concerning.

"Iris—"

"I—" Our words are cut off when a tepid woosh of air hits my back. I jump in surprise for the second time in minutes and turn to meet the intense hazel gaze and towering figure of Wilder Quinn.

"Ah, Iris. Here you are," he says gruffly. "We've been waiting for you."

Chapter Four

Mateo

After meeting August, I didn't think it was possible to fall in love at first sight again. I thought I'd used up my fate allotments, and if by chance we found an Omega that fulfilled our pack, it would be the kind of love that was nurtured and grew like a flower in spring.

But all it took was looking into Iris Walker's silver-grey eyes and touching her soft skin to believe that she's *mine*. My Alpha is practically clawing out from under my skin, begging me to touch her again, to throw her into a shower and scrub her clean of the awful de-scenting pray and whatever else she's got caked on to block her scent. Confirm what my instincts are already saying even if I can't be 100 percent sure.

Mierda. Augie is never going to let me hear the end of it when I tell him. I was just teasing him about crushing on this Omega for so many years through a screen, but now that I've met her, felt her presence near me, I know I'm going to be as equally obsessed with her as he is. It makes me wonder if my mate's instincts somehow knew what she could be to us, even through a TV screen.

My gaze finds Augie's as I walk through the set door behind Iris. He's standing next to Jett, his green eyes locked on the Omega and skin already flushed with nerves. I can't wait to see how he reacts when they shake hands. I wonder if he'll feel the same way I do right now, even if I know he already will.

Then there's my other pack members. They tend to be more guarded in their feelings and a bit dense. Without her scent I don't know if they'll have the reaction I just did to her.

Wilder stands next to Augie with Jett on the other side of him. He doesn't look at me, but to the Omega, an annoyed pulse coming through our bond, no doubt from our tardiness. My Alpha almost growled when he interrupted us, but it's good that he did. Regardless of if my instincts want to pick Iris up and throw her over my shoulder, taking us to a private spot where I can fuck her seven ways to Sunday, that would be highly inadvisable. A lawsuit waiting to happen. And my pack would kill me without talking to them about my discovery first. Or what I hope I discovered.

I don't like that Iris didn't seem to react to my scent. There's some de-scenter the crew sprays in the air that dampens the many scents here so it's not overwhelming to everyone working, but she should have been able to pick mine up with how close we were.

The image of mi conejita scrunching her nose consumes my thoughts. She did look like a cute little bunny every time she made the action, but now I'm wondering if her Omega didn't care for my honey scent. It would be odd considering I attract enough bees to pollinate my hive on the regular if I so choose.

"I see you met Mateo, our cinematographer," Wilder addresses Iris as we come to a stop in front of the three of them.

I shake my inappropriate thoughts away as Iris holds her hands in front of her, fingers gripped together with what I can only guess are nerves. I want to take her hand and assure her she has nothing to be nervous about, but I don't blame her with the way Wilder is coming across.

He's an intimidating Alpha at six foot five and covered in tattoos. I've joked before that he looks like a biker and a rockstar had a baby, much to his annoyance. But once you get to know him, and if you're lucky enough that he lets you in, he's a teddy bear at heart. He's also a damn good director and the best Prime our pack could ask for.

"Yes," her answer comes out a bit shaky so she clears her throat and tries again. "Yes, I did."

"Good," Wilder replies. I try to read him or see if I can feel a spike of any sort of emotion through the bond other than the fading annoyance, but he stays level. But that's not unusual for him. He's good at remaining professional no matter the circumstance.

"We're running a tight ship as you may know," he continues. "This isn't how I normally like to do things, but we really have to jump right in or we'll fall behind. That means we don't have much time for pleasantries. Hopefully we'll get to know each other as the shoot goes on and during meal breaks."

What Wilder doesn't know is I very much plan for our pack to get to know her, but I keep that to myself for now. I don't need my Alpha going wild and making things awkward. I need to remain calm while we work and figure the rest out later. Thank the gods I'm good at restraint.

Iris dips her chin and I notice she's relieved by his rushing and lack of niceties, because the grip she has on her hands is easing.

"I understand, sorry I came in late."

"That was my doing," I cut in. Their eyes turn on me, including Iris's. "I scared her and sent her into a coughing fit then offered her regular coffee like an asshole."

That's not exactly what happened but I don't want my pack to think she took too much time to show up on her first day of shooting. She was right outside when I ran into her.

"Here," Augie's warm voice cuts in. He holds out a water bottle I didn't see in his hand and she looks down at it. "It's unopened."

"It's okay—"

"Please, it's yours now."

"Thanks," she says softly, her hand reaching out to take the offered drink. My eyes fall to the bottle and I see the moment her fingers brush my Beta's. Iris gasps and he pulls back without thinking, the actions causing the water bottle to drop to the floor.

"Shoot," Iris proclaims, and I know what's about to happen before it does.

She bends down to grab the dropped plastic bottle at the same time my mate does. Their foreheads collide and they both curse, yet they go back in for the bottle like kittens over a ball of yarn. Just before their heads whack again, Wilder's tattooed hand strikes out like a snake and grabs Augie's shoulder, stopping him from hitting her again. There's even a brief second where I think he growls, and not in a normal angry way but in a way that an Alpha protects his Omega.

My eyes lift to his but he's not looking at me. His narrowed gaze is on Iris as she stands with the water bottle in her hand and her other hand rubbing her forehead under her dark bangs. Meanwhile Jett stands on the other side of Wilder with his arms over his chest, brow knitted in confusion as he stares at our Prime, obviously having heard the growl.

Hmm, that was interesting, now wasn't it?

Augie's reaction I can understand, and Iris clearly felt something when she touched my mate.

And Wilder…

I tap further into our pack bond. There's no denying he's confused by what he just did. I can feel Augie's embarrassment, Jett's curiosity, and an undercurrent of attraction that I believe to be coming from all of us.

Could these reactions to Iris simply be because not only is she a very attractive Omega and exactly our type with her generous curves and dark hair, but she's unbonded? Many of the Omegas we've worked with, Molly included, had packs and bond marks that makeup had to cover up for shoots—but not Iris.

Mine.

My spine straightens. I guess my Alpha disagrees with me on that. I feel his anger at just the idea she's only a random unbonded Omega. I can understand why too, because our pack has worked with them before, and of course many cross our paths outside of work, and I've never felt like this. And I've never heard Wilder growl like that over something as simple as a clumsy head collision. Jett hasn't given much of an outward reaction, but the way he's looking at her now, eyes focused, and the attraction in the bond, he's feeling something too.

"I'm so sorry," Augie mutters, snapping my attention back to him. He's standing at his full height, pushing his glasses up his nose. "Are you okay, Iris?"

His eyes draw to the Omega's hand rubbing her forehead and she immediately drops it. I force my hands to stay at my sides to stop myself from taking her in my arms and checking her over.

"I'm fine," she exhales, holding the water bottle in both hands now. "I swear I'm usually not this clumsy. Sorry."

"Don't be, it was my fault," Augie adds.

Iris opens her mouth as if she wants to debate but Jett clears his throat. "We should get started before Augie ends up apologizing ten more times."

The light southern twang of his accent is more prominent than normal, and there's a pulse of curiosity through the bond. This time from not only me but from Augie and Wilder.

Jett's lived in California since he was seventeen and is thirty now like the rest of our pack. He did a lot of work to get rid of his accent for roles unless it's needed, and it tends to only come out when he's stressed or laying it on thick for women he's trying to bed if they think it's charming. But I don't think it's either of those things at the moment. The slip felt natural, like a wall came down that made him feel at ease with her to show the real him only our pack sees.

Mierda, mierda, mierda! I think Iris really could be our Omega! My heart pounds in my chest and I wish more than anything I could take my pack and Iris into a room, explain what's going on, and ask to court her, but that would all be insane. There's also the fact we're surrounded by a crew and have responsibilities that trump my Alpha instincts right now.

"That sounds good," Iris says with a small smile, silver eyes alight.

There's an awkward pause before Wilder claps his hands, making both her and Augie jump slightly at its suddenness.

"I'll restart us." His gruff tone is laced with enough of his Alpha bark that we all stand at attention. "I think we know each other's names at this point but I'm Wilder, this is August, he's the brilliant writer behind *Knotting Hill*, and he'll be on set with us for the next month. I'm not sure if I'd mentioned it on our call, but he'll also be my assistant director for this shoot."

Iris's silver gaze travels to my mate's; he's rubbing the back of his neck in the way he does when he feels shy and nervous. He'd probably be gripping the water bottle between his hands like she is had he not given it to her.

"That's me," he says, his voice a tad squeaky. It's fucking adorable and I feel my amusement along with my fellow packmates flow through the bond.

Iris dips her chin. "It's nice to meet you, August."

"You can call me Augie if you like."

"Augie," she says, eyelids fluttering and skin pinkening. "You can call me Iris."

He chuckles and my gaze catches Wilder and Jett's. I know they see her flush and the way she already appears starry eyed for Augie. I think mi conejita has a bit of a crush on our Beta, one that pre-dates their meeting like his does for her. I store that information away alongside everything else I've learned in these last minutes.

"Then of course you met Mateo, our cinematographer. You'll get to know his crew as we go," Wilder says.

"Mateo is fine." I smile at her when her attention turns to me. Though I want to say she can call me Alpha too if she wants. Or anything, really.

Iris grins softly and her nostrils flare on an inhale at the same time mine do. Once again I only get the smells of my pack and the de-scenting agents she has on, but her nose scrunches like before. She covers it by turning away and bringing the back of her finger up to rub it daintily like she has an itch. Augie stares into the side of my head and I look over at him. His face is confused and I know he saw whatever that was, but I don't have an answer for him.

"Lastly," Wilder continues. "We have Jett, your leading man. Your other costars should be around at lunch and Jett or one of the PAs can introduce you."

"It's nice to finally meet you, Iris." Jett steps toward her a miniscule amount so as to not come off threatening, his natural charm of an A-list celebrity and Alpha radiating off him like a magical aura. His accent is nowhere to be found now.

"You too, Jett." She smiles—one that forms dimples on her cheeks that I didn't realize she had. She's captivating, and I'm seriously wondering why we didn't fight the investors harder to hire her over Molly in the first place. And by the look on Jett's face, I think he agrees.

His blue eyes have dropped to Iris's lips, his gaze zeroed in on them like her saying his name was the best thing he's ever heard. A pulse of deep attraction comes from his end of the pack bond and the air pulls tight around us.

Something interesting is definitely happening between my pack and Iris. And I know that if I don't move us from the spot we'll all stand here until one of us drags Iris away and to the nearest private room.

I rub my hands together. "Now that we all know each other, should we block and test the lighting?"

"Yes," Wilder agrees, his voice strained rather than his normal director-like tone. "Let's get started."

Chapter Five

Iris

The blocking and lighting over the last hour have gone well enough. I held my breath nearly the entire time while Wilder directed us, Mateo and his team did slight adjustments, and Jett and I did what they asked of us, thankfully with no touching yet. I even managed to keep my nose from scrunching if I breathed in too hard. I still hate the smell, but I'm glad it's working along with the de-scenter spray and deodorant.

Honestly, it's a small miracle, because being on set with Pack Quinn is intense. When I was introduced to them, it was more difficult than I thought it would be to stand together, all of them staring at me in close proximity. Not only are they all more attractive in person, their energy as a pack is electric. It's not often that I'm surrounded by members of the same pack, unless you count my dads and mom when I drop in for visits to Seattle. I forgot how intense it can be, and Pack Quinn, they're as intense as it gets.

Wilder especially. He's massively tall, to the point my five-foot-ten frame felt small next to his, and that's rare for me. His dark eyes and growly voice had more than my toes curling, and I'm blessed my Omega stayed calm. Which is odd. I expected after the way she acted when Mateo touched me to go feral. I felt her a little when Augie, who's hotter than Clark Kent by far, and I touched, but the pain of bonking our heads together stopped me from truly processing the spark I swear I felt.

Then there's Jett. I've never had an issue keeping it professional with costars, but if I let myself cross any lines, I would for him. His dark blond hair, the shade of wet sand, faded tight at the sides with curls left loose on top—messy, yet far too sexy to be an accident—makes me want to run my fingers through it.

I didn't realize he had a southern twang to his voice. He did in a cowboy film once but otherwise I've never heard it. I won't lie and say I didn't almost imagine him calling me darlin', but I'll imagine that later when I'm in the comfort of my nest and after the shoot is done.

Geeze. If this is where my mind is traveling to now, I can't even imagine what would have happened if I was able to scent them. No actually, I do know. It would have been bad, especially since I'm already thinking of them in ways I shouldn't when I'm literally on set with them and I'm here to do my job.

Professional, Iris. We're going to be professional and we're not going to have any Omega biology mishaps.

"Do you two feel good?" Wilder asks Jett and I as Mateo walks off to grab another quick cup of "go-go" juice while Augie watches on with his laptop on his lap in Video Village where Sadie is patiently sitting and texting on her phone. The few times I've looked over at him, sometimes I catch his eye and he blushes. It's sweet and endearing, and I wonder if he has a crush on me like I have on him.

"I feel good. Iris?" Jett asks, his accent nowhere to be found now.

I dip my chin, ignoring how disappointed I am that he didn't use it. I want to ask him why he actively tries to hide it, because it sounded natural before. But now's not the time.

"Yep, I'm solid," I say.

Jett's blue gaze studies me. When our eyes lock, my skin prickles and the sounds of the people milling about on set fade into the distance as I become entranced by him like I did with Mateo earlier. A tugging sensation in the middle of my stomach appears out of nowhere and it takes everything in me not to step closer to him or inhale long and hard in hopes I can scent him.

My chest tightens on a whimper at the same time the clearing of Wilder's throat cuts through my haze. I swallow hard and will the abrupt appearance of my Omega down again before I embarrass myself. I went the entire time while we lit and blocked without incident, and now this?

I exhale a shallow breath as Jett and I turn to Wilder, the big Alpha's eyes slightly narrowed as he observes us.

His lips part like he's going to say something but then he clears his throat again before speaking. "Quick rehearsal for the first shot and then we'll roll right into the first take."

"Great," Jett and I echo at the same time.

Wilder darts his focus between us once more before he says something about alerting the crew and to take our marks that we blocked out. In this scene, Hugh enters Juliette's bookshop for the first time and begins to browse. He picks up a book that's particularly bad and she stops him from reading it. They end up flirting a bit and getting close to kissing before he finally leaves the shop.

I'm both excited and terrified about being that close to his mouth, but I'm going to have to get used to it considering we have a kissing scene tomorrow that I need to prepare both myself and my demon Omega for. In a week's time it will only get more intense when we have a sex scene, but I'll cross that bridge when we come to it.

There's a light sensation on my arm and look down to where Jett's masculine fingers are touching my bicep. While Mateo's touch felt like fire, and Augie's felt like an electric spark, Jett's is like jumping into refreshing ocean water.

My body reacts immediately, goosebumps breaking out over my flesh. I bite the inside of my cheek and breathe slowly so I don't scrunch my nose and get called a bunny by him too before I finally look back into his eyes.

"Iris," Jett says.

Time slows down and I can't blink, can't look away. Once again I'm captivated by him and the masculine planes of his bearded face. I could try to blame it on his natural hot actor charm that draws me, but this feels like more for whatever reason.

"Yes?" I manage to ask, though my voice sounds an octave higher than it usually is.

I expect him to drop his hand, but he doesn't. "I wanted to say before we start shooting that I'm glad you're playing my Juliette."

My Juliette. It's my character's name but my Omega who's decided to make herself known, *again*, preens as if he said I'm *his Omega*. I quietly remind her that I was the second choice but she doesn't care; she only cares that she has the attention and touch of a very beguiling Alpha who doesn't have an Omega.

When I don't immediately say anything he continues, "You're an incredible actor. I've seen your work, and I think we're going to be great together on screen."

And off screen.

Goddamn, Omega brain! I ignore the voice and smile, attempting to also ignore his touch still on my arm, one that's starting to heat my skin the longer it stays connected to me. Like a pot of water slowly coming to a boil.

"Thank you, Jett. I'm really happy to be here."

I brush at the bangs on my forehead as he drops his hand from my arm. Before I can miss his touch, he places his finger under my chin and turns my head toward his, brushing my bangs away like I just did. A frown mars his masculine features and my fingers itch to reach out and take him in my arms, to comfort him until he's no longer frowning.

"You're getting a bruise." A sound akin to a growl rumbles from his strong chest and two things happen inside me at once—I shiver and heat pools low in my belly. The kind of heat that could very much get me in trouble if I let it build.

The big, tattooed Alpha growled like this earlier, too, my Omega so lovingly reminds me.

Yeah, I know, but like Wilder's presence, his growl felt calming and protective more than anything else. Either way, any kind of growls and the way they make me feel are not acceptable right now and I can't think about how they make me feel at all.

I grit my teeth and step back from Jett so his hand is forced to drop down. "It's okay." I touch my forehead. It's a tiny bit tender but if there's a bruise it should be gone by tomorrow. Omegas and Alphas heal quickly, a perk of biology and especially useful for Omegas when in heats or during childbirth.

Jett slides his tongue over his front teeth. "It's not okay. Augie!"

The Beta's head snaps up toward us from his laptop, his spine straightening from the bite of Jett's bark. My spine also stiffens, even though his anger isn't directed at me.

"Get hair and makeup for Iris and some ice."

Augie gets up from his chair and leaves without looking at me. I take a second to glance at Sadie and she's eyeing me with questions and concern, but I just shrug. I have no idea why Jett's acting this way. He went from being sweet to an Alphahole in two seconds flat.

I turn my attention back to Jett. His pupils are slightly dilated, the blue of them more like stormy seas rather than a calm blue ocean. His fists are clenched and he's staring at my forehead in anger. Jett's growl slowly intensifies and I debate what to do.

It's been a long time since I've been around an angry Alpha, or at least one that looks on the brink of losing control. It's odd because we just met, and while I haven't seen it, I'm sure the bruise is hardly there and can be covered by makeup and my hair. He shouldn't be reacting like this. But it's like some weird switch flipped in his brain.

"Jett?" I try, but his only answer is to get closer to me and inhale.

Oh no, that's not good.

I tell my body to take a step back but I can't move, my Omega doesn't want me to move. I guess I have to use my voice instead.

"Jett, I swear I'm fine." My voice is calm and easy. "It doesn't even hurt."

The muscles beneath the shirt he's wearing flex, and the veins in his throat bulge. His head dips down and his nostrils flare as he tries to scent me again. When he can't, the growl in his throat deepens, and his Alpha's frustration seeps out of him along with it. I go to say his name again, maybe even try addressing his Alpha, but thankfully I don't have to.

"Jett!" Wilder's bark is loud and the whole set goes quiet. "Come here."

At first the Alpha next to me doesn't move, but after a long moment of staring between the packmates, he gives me one last long pained glance before he stalks off with Wilder, Augie, and Mateo following behind them. My body moves to follow like a puppy after its owners, but thankfully I'm stopped by hair and makeup.

Shit, what was that?

Alphas, my Omega pouts. Yeah, I know. They're Alphas. But they aren't *my* Alphas, and they can't be my Alphas. I pop my shoulders back and collect myself, following a Beta makeup artist to a chair. I let her cover the bruise Jett freaked out about and another Beta touch up my hair. Sadie approaches me once they're out of sight and I tug her to the bathroom a PA pointed out to us since the Alpha's aren't back yet.

"What was that?" she asks when the door is closed and I make sure nobody is inside with us. "I thought Jett was going to go all caveman for a second there and Wilder—he's scary."

"I don't know," I huff. "But I think I should refresh the neutralizer and put on more of that deodorant. The more, the better."

CHAPTER SIX

Wilder

"JETT, I NEED YOU to calm down," I demand once my pack is safely in a holding room with the door closed.

He threads his fingers through his hair violently, pacing the length of the small space as Augie and Mateo flank my sides. I've never seen him like this before, and the way he looks right now, the only comparison I can think of is a feral wolf in a cage. That's not good.

"Jett!" I bark loudly, lacing all my dominance into his name. He stops his pacing, turning to face me and our pack. His blue eyes are practically black, and if I didn't know any better, I'd say he was on the verge of rut. The last time he had one was two years ago, and none of us know what triggered it.

We were at some fancy Halloween party in the Beverly Hills. One moment he was fine and the next he was lost. Thankfully Augie was able to take care of him and no cops needed to be called. If they had, he would have been put into a padded cell until he calmed down. An awful experience no Alpha wants to go through. After that he's been on stronger rut blockers, the same dose I am for safety reasons, and he should have had a shot this morning before coming on set.

"Did you not get your rut blocker?"

"I did," he grits out. "But I'm not going into a rut."

"He's not," Mateo assures, stepping forward. "This is different." He holds up his hands in surrender, tipping his neck to the side so Jett's Alpha knows he means no harm.

A low growl reverberates from Jett and he snarls. Regardless of how he's feeling, I know he understands that Maren would never harm him. But with that said, I've never seen him react to an Omega like this. Let alone one who we can't even scent.

Iris has on so many de-scenting agents you'd think she was dipped in a vat of them. It agitated my Alpha—a fact I've been trying to ignore since I normally wouldn't care—but after seeing Jett like this I'm glad for it.

"Can you take a breath for me, compa?" Mateo asks. "I know you're not going into a rut, but if you don't calm down you just might. It smells like sour lemons in here and my eyes are watering." The last part is said with a teasing affection that only he can achieve.

Jett fists his hands at his sides, knuckles white. For a second I don't think he's going to do it but he sucks in a breath, his growl fading with the inhale.

"That's it. Take a few more."

Mateo lowers his hands as Jett does what he says. My packmate blinks and every time his eyes open his dark pupils retract, his irises returning to their normal shade of blue.

My gaze finds Augie's while his mate continues to calm Jett down. I can feel him pumping his calming Beta energy through our bond, and I appreciate him for it.

"You good?" I mouth to him. He nods, but I can tell he isn't. Whatever happened between him and Iris earlier and now this, has him anxious. I want to say I'm fine but that wouldn't be true. Since the moment Iris walked into our sphere only an hour ago, my pack has been off kilter. I thought maybe I made it up, but something is clearly wrong.

"Jett," Mateo says.

I turn my attention back to the two Alpha's. The scent in the air no longer smells of acidic lemons, but I can still smell Jett's normal tangy lemon pheromones with their sweet yet sour edge. It's concerning because that means whatever happened most likely caused him to burn through his high dose of rut blockers.

And I most certainly should not be able to smell him at this strength with the de-scenters the crew sprays in the air.

"I'm sorry," Jett respires. He runs a hand through his hair in frustration. "I don't know what came over me."

I take an easy step toward them, pushing my Alpha down as far as I can right now given I too feel on edge. Jett is still walking a careful line of control, and I don't want to accidentally set him off again.

Jett's worried eyes find mine and I keep my hands in my pockets with my chin dipped down. I won't give him my throat but his Alpha will see I mean well.

"Do you have any idea what happened?" I ask.

"I think it's my fault," Augie answers instead.

The three of us turn to him, his features sullen despite his continuous pumping of calming energy through the bond.

"What do you mean, mi amor?" Mateo asks.

"Jett's Alpha went into a rage because Iris was hurt."

The growl I loosed earlier builds back at the mention of Iris and hurt in the same sentence. It's a ridiculous reaction, just like the reaction earlier was ridiculous. I'd chalked it up to my Alpha wanting to protect an Omega, that I would have acted like that for anyone. Now I'm doubting that more than I already was.

Augie comes closer to us so his arm touches Mateo's and his gaze is locked on Jett's. "I didn't mean to hurt her, Alpha. I'm still mad at myself for it."

Our Beta always knows the right things to say and do. Addressing Jett's Alpha directly seems to have done the trick. Jett's jaw relaxes, his muscles easing further and eyes clear. He's back to normal now, or at least as close as he can be after that. Alpha rage can often lead to a rut or worse, an Alpha going feral. It's rare, but has happened. Thank fuck this crisis was overcome because losing Jett to that would hurt us all.

"It's okay, Augie," he exhales, relaxing his hands at his sides. "My reaction was uncalled for. I'm sorry," he looks between Mateo and I, "To you both as well."

I clap him on the shoulder and squeeze. "Nothing bad happened and that's the most important thing. But I can't let you go back out there if you think you'll lose your composure again."

There's a lull of silence as the four of us look between each other. Our pack bond is crackling with anxiety. It's not good that Jett doesn't immediately say yes.

"I'll have the set doctor come and give you another dose of rut blockers to be on the safe side. For now, we'll shoot close ups and singles of Iris until you feel confident. How does that sound?"

Mateo shakes his head. "I don't think rut blockers are the solution."

"I understand his Alpha was enraged, but it smells like a goddamn lemon grove in here. Jett, if I didn't know any better, I'd say you were a perfuming Omega."

Jett narrows his eyes. "It does not."

I run a hand over my beard. "Trust me, it does. And need I remind you, a rage can trigger a rut."

"I'm not going into a rut!"

"Both of you, stop!" Mateo yells.

Maybe I should have had more tact in how I spoke about my observation, but Jett's lemon keeps getting stronger, stronger than I've smelled it before. Even when he's succumbed to a rut or we've helped an Omega through a heat together. The more I think about it, the odder I find it. His scent shouldn't be this fucking strong and the rut blocker will hopefully subdue his out of whack pheromones.

"It's the best solution," I argue.

Mateo throws up his hands and mutters, "Pinche idiota, alfa."

I grunt. I am acting like an idiot, but I'm on edge and if my Alpha had his way, he'd skip everything I suggested and knock Jett out, hopefully resetting him back to before Iris walked into the room. I need him acting like himself before I put him safely in a scene with her.

"If not rut blockers, then what?" I ask. "I'm open to a solution if you have one."

Mateo clucks his tongue against his teeth. "You really don't know what's happening?"

"Mateo," I say with an agitated edge to my voice. "He had an episode of Alpha rage."

"Yes, but it's more than that."

I raise an annoyed brow at him. "Would you tell us then? We don't have time for guessing games."

He sighs. "I was hoping you'd all put it together."

"Put what together?" Jett asks, his tone aggravated now.

Augie sucks in a loud breath of air, his eyes widening comically in shock before a blast of awe and elation comes from his end of the bond.

Mateo smirks. "Mi amor figured it out."

A growl builds in my chest and my mint scent spikes, the pheromones so sharp they almost make me cough.

"Easy there, compa."

"Mateo." My anger builds and it takes everything in me to pull it back. Fuck, it's like whatever happened to Jett is contagious.

The corner of Mateo's lip lifts and I grit my teeth. I love my pack, but sometimes my fellow Alpha's are great at pushing my buttons. Especially Mateo when he wants to; it's part of our dynamic.

"Tell him, baby," Augie urges.

Mateo's dark brown eyes focus on mine, the amused twinkle in them turning serious in a way that makes my stomach bottom out.

"Iris Walker is our Omega."

The air is sucked from my lungs and it's as if cold water is dumped on my head. Jett is still beside me, and I don't have to look at him to know he's as shocked to hear Mateo's words as I am. Augie remains excited and in awe, his usual soothing energy a mix of the emotions.

"But that's impossible," I say.

"Is it?" Mateo pushes back.

"We can't even scent her," Jett reminds him.

"Which is a good thing, because I don't believe even Wilder's bark would have pulled you from that room if you had, Jett. I think we'd have carried her off like a wild pack of wolves given the way we've been reacting to her even without her scent. We've probably scared the shit out of her with how weird we've been acting and that last display."

My Alpha doesn't like that notion at all. A rough thrum builds in my chest and escapes before I can stop it.

My pack stares wide-eyed at me, and I look down at my chest like it betrayed me.

"Case in point. She's not even here and your Alpha just purred for her," Mateo says with a smug tone. "Little rusty sounding, compa."

I shut my purr down that did in fact sound like a rusty engine, mortified by my own behavior.

"That doesn't mean she's ours." As soon as I utter the words I feel sick and my Alpha bangs against my ribs as if he's trying to get out to beat me up for saying something so ridiculous.

I rub at my sternum, and Mateo places his hand on my arm, gripping my bicep tight.

"Wilder, I know it seems hard to believe that she'd walk into our lives like this, but my Alpha knew the moment he saw her." He places his free hand over his heart, mirroring me. "I thought it was crazy at first too, but it's clear to me now after all this. Most importantly, my Alpha, my heart, knows."

My heart thuds against my hand; my Alpha that's normally hard around the edges, softening at Mateo's admission.

"You may not believe it yet, but your Alpha did the moment he growled out there." He pulls back from me and looks at Jett. "You went near full Alpha rage at just the sight of a small bruise on her forehead, not something you'd do for just anyone. And I think your scent is strong because your Alpha wants her to recognize you. And mi amor"—he moves to cup Augie's cheek—"I think there's a reason you've always felt drawn to Iris. You may not be an Alpha but you knew all along just seeing her through a screen. And I think you felt something when you met her, yes?"

He nods. "When her fingers brushed mine, it felt like something clicked inside me. A missing piece. But I didn't want to get my hopes up about anything. But, I think you're right, baby."

Jett drags a hand over his face. "You realize how insane this is, right?"

"Do you think Augie and I are both wrong?" Mateo asks.

"My Alpha agrees with you both," Jett says readily, his southern accent slipping through like it did with Iris earlier—another odd thing to add to the odd bank of today. "But as mentioned, we can't scent her. How can we know for sure?"

"I trust my Alpha. If he says she's mine, she is," Mateo says.

"Ours," Augie interjects.

Mateo takes his hand and squeezes, their eyes locking as words they don't say pass between them before Mateo corrects, "Ours."

Jett bumps my shoulder and I meet his gaze. He lifts a brow at me, and I know he's waiting for me to speak. I'm the Prime of this pack, and I'm not going to lie and say I'm feeling off center right now.

If all of this is true, how did my Alpha not immediately recognize Iris as ours like Mateo's did?

I don't say it out loud often, but I've wanted an Omega for our pack since we formed and bonded. I may look like a man who'd scoff at romance on the outside, but I came from a loving scent-matched pack with a male and female Alpha who adored my Omega mother. I've wanted what they had since I was a teenager.

When we didn't find our Omega in college, I'd turned my focus to my pack and our careers, hoping we'd find them at some point. Even if scent matches are rare. Over the years I'd stuffed my romantic dream to the back of my mind, our success making it hard to date and even harder now with Jett's continual rising star. I resigned myself to one-night stands and the occasional heat clinic volunteer alongside my pack.

In my dreams, the moment I met my Omega, I would have known.

"I can feel you beating yourself up," Augie says.

"I—" My words catch and I think of what to say. I don't like being weak in front of them. I'm their leader, the one they look to for answers. I don't like that I don't have any.

I tensely exhale. "I'm just frustrated with myself that I'm doubting your words. It just doesn't make sense."

"You rely on your nose too much. I have no doubt in my mind that if you could scent her, we'd be having a different conversation," Mateo says.

"Maybe so, but wouldn't she react to finding her pack if this was true? We may not be able to scent her, but she can still smell us. There's no way she would have missed Jett's pheromones."

"I had the same thought, but I think I figured it out. Her Omega kept trying to scent me, but every time she did her nose scrunched like a rabbit."

I mull over his words and the moments we spent with Iris. The way she's covered her scent, how she didn't react to us how a scent match or scent-sensitive Omega would, and I do remember her scrunching her nose. There's only one thing that could make her do that, I know because I used them in my teens when I played Rugby. I scrunch my nose just thinking about that sterile smell. But it was better than smelling a bunch of sweaty guys.

"She's using a nasal scent neutralizer," I say.

"Bingo."

"Why would she do that?" Jett asks. "I don't think I've met an actor who's used them on set before."

"Maybe she's more comfortable with them," I say, making a mental note to dig a bit more into Iris Walker tonight. We always make our sets comfortable spaces for any actor and designation, but now I'm curious if Iris has had bad experiences on set before that we aren't aware of. Jett is right that it's unusual for anyone to choose to inhale that disgusting spray.

"Iris may not have reacted like our pack has to her, but I think her Omega knows on some level too," Augie says.

"How so?" Jett asks.

"She felt something when she touched me. It's why she gasped and we dropped the water. Then when you three were blocking and lighting, I saw the way she was entranced by all of you. How the four of you moved together easily, and how she fit so quickly despite the start we've had. There's something there for her too, even if she doesn't know it yet."

The image of Iris standing next to Jett on set, Mateo lighting them to perfection comes to mind. It was easy working with her so far, but I didn't think much of it. I was doing my best to be professional. I have no doubt I came off a little angry now that I think about it. I'll have to apologize to her, make sure she knows she's safe with me, with us. Maybe after a few days she'll feel comfortable to ease up on the de-scenters and neutralizers.

My Alpha grunts in approval, the dark-haired beauty fully taking over my brain. I didn't truly allow myself to appreciate the Omega before. Like I said, I was trying to remain professional, but she's perfect. More than perfect.

Kind, hardworking, tall and voluptuous, with hips that I could grip on to and not worry about hurting as she took my knot. It's the kind of body that's made for me, for my pack.

Mine.

My heart stops in my chest at the word. My pack can't hear my thoughts but no doubt they felt possessiveness that just burst through the bond.

Mateo chuckles. "You're getting it now."

Jett blows a breath through his tight lips. "What the hell do we do with this information? We have a movie to shoot."

Different options come to mind. In a normal situation, we'd ask Iris if we could officially court her. It sounds dated, but it's what packs do when they want to potentially have an Omega join their pack. We show the Omega what we can offer them, the pack they can have to take care and cherish them.

"If we could court her, that would be the best option," I say.

"Why can't we?" Augie asks.

"She technically works for us so there's a conflict of interest. On top of that we don't have time to truly court her. She could also say no and then she'd be uncomfortable the rest of the shoot."

"She won't say no," Mateo says, his voice carrying the kind of authority that tells me his Alpha has taken over.

If I didn't have to lead this pack and a movie to direct, I have no doubt I would have said the same. But it's true, we all just met, none of us know what she smells like and it's clear she doesn't know what we smell like. We're going off our reactions and instincts alone, including the deep-seated hope we've pushed aside that one day we would find our Omega.

"You can't be sure of that, Mateo. We don't even know her," I say. Though the words feel sour on my tongue as I speak them.

He blinks, fists flexing at his sides. Augie places a hand on his mate's back and rubs.

"I know you're right, but my Alpha says you're wrong." Mateo sighs.

"I get it. I do."

"Look, we can pull this back a little, yeah?" Jett interjects.

"Meaning?" I ask.

"There's no need for a declaration right now," Jett says. "We've waited this long for an Omega who fits our pack, not one chasing fame or money. I can't explain it, but my Alpha knows Iris isn't like the others. Let's work with her, get to know her, and if we still feel the same by the end of the shoot, we'll make it official and ask to court her. We don't know the scent match yet, but I trust Mateo on this one, and my instincts say it won't be an issue."

"I think that's the best way to go, too." Mateo nods with finality.

"Same," Augie adds.

I comb my hand through my hair. I may be used to thinking logically, but like my pack, my instincts are riding me. My Alpha is in nothing but agreement with them, even if all this seems like too much of a dream come true. Like a movie more than reality.

Mine.

I rub my chest as I stare back at my pack, the hope clear in their eyes. I can't disagree with them, neither can my Alpha.

"Alright." I finally nod in agreement. "We're all on the same page moving forward then?" The three of them smile brightly back at me and dip their chins, our bond buzzing with hope and happiness, assuring me this is the right path forward.

I turn my focus to Jett, lacing dominance into my next words. "What happened out there, can't happen again."

"I know. I was caught off guard, but I'm good now." He looks at the rest of our pack with determined eyes. "I swear it."

"If you feel anything at all, you get off set. Just walk off."

"I will," he promises.

"You good, Mateo?"

"I'm good."

"Augie?"

He smiles gratefully at me, but he knows I'll always include him. He may not be an Alpha, but he's loved Iris before he knew her. His Beta clearly reacts to her, even without her scent. That means something to me.

He smirks. "I'll make sure you all don't embarrass me."

That makes us all chuckle. "It's settled then. Let's get back out there. We're behind, but if we put in an extra hour tonight we can catch up."

I clap Jett on the back and he smiles softly, our gazes locking. In all the time I've known him, since our first week of college, I've never seen him look this hopeful before. I knew we both wanted an Omega, but I guess I didn't realize he'd been craving it as much and as deeply as I have, especially after his stalker and Omegas chasing his money.

"What about you?" he asks.

"I'm good," I assure him.

"If Iris is ours—"

"She is," Mateo and Augie say at the same time.

"If everything goes well, things are going to change," Jett says.

I smile despite the near absurdity of it all, but he's right.

"Good," I say with conviction. My pack is everything to me. The life we've built is everything to me. But there's always been a missing piece. One we thought we may never have.

If Iris is that piece like my Alpha, and my pack thinks she is, then I'm going to do everything I can to make sure she knows she's ours. But first, we get through this shoot. Once that's done, we'll make our intentions known. Getting to know Iris as friends will have to be enough for now.

CHAPTER SEVEN

Jett

Omega.

Yeah, buddy. I know she's an Omega, I say in my mind, keeping my Alpha calm and placated. I ended up popping a low dose rut blocker to be on the safe side after my rage episode, but being around Iris is how I imagine a sailor near a Siren. The long column of her throat is calling to me. I want to feel her pulse under my lips, to scent mark her and press my nose against her scent gland.

I've been doing everything in my power to *not* imagine what she smells like, but standing close to her for nearly twelve hours in an enclosed set is not helping me. Despite hating the smell of her de-scenting agents, I'm grateful that they're there so I don't go into a rut.

"Alright, let's get set for the last shot of the day, everyone," Wilder calls.

A couple of the crew clap and begin resetting for the shot. I have no idea what time it is, but I know it's late. Being on a set lit for daytime makes it look like it's the middle of the day, but it's probably nearing midnight. Despite the long day, however, and my "mishap" earlier, I don't feel tired.

I look over at Iris who's sitting in a chair next to me after our last makeup and hair touch up. She smiles softly, my heart palpitating in my chest. I know until we scent her we can't be 100 percent sure she's ours, but in my heart I know she's our scent-matched Omega—our mate. My Alpha wants to purr in agreement, but unlike Wilder I'm able to keep it in.

My gaze holds hers, and I like that she doesn't look away. Her silvery-grey eyes remind me of the moon, and I find myself wanting to know what she's thinking for the millionth time today. Day one of the shoot has gone off without another hitch, our chemistry is off the charts, and I'm an idiot for not pushing harder to get her hired over Molly to begin with.

When I saw her audition, she was perfect, and I was pulled in by her sensitivity and the gentle way her round face and clear eyes portrayed Juliette in the scene. But our investors won the fight to hire Molly.

I wish we could go back in time and choose her from the jump. We would have done a chemistry test together and found her sooner—the Omega my pack has been waiting for. The Omega I wasn't sure we'd ever find. I'd resigned myself to hookups and heat clinics, but not anymore. Meeting Iris has shifted something inside me, and I know without a doubt, even without the confirmation of scent or knowing her for longer than half a day, I'd do anything for her. I can only hope she feels the same when she recognizes us as hers.

"You doing okay?" I ask her.

Iris nods, tucking a piece of hair behind her ear. She's been careful to not touch her bangs again, which I appreciate. Makeup covered the small bruise that made me lose my goddamn mind, but I know it's there, and it's good my Alpha can no longer see it.

"I'm good, excited for a shower and sleep though," she replies.

"Eager to get rid of me already?"

The apples of her cheeks that makeup refreshed with a bit of light pink blush deepens in color and she turns, leaning closer to me from her chair. "No, no, that's not what I meant—you're great, *so* great—"

I touch her arm, my Alpha pushing me to sooth her and stop her rambling. "I was kidding." I smile at her, her praise heating me up inside. "I know it's been a long day. I could use a shower, too."

Iris laughs under her breath. "Sorry, I ramble when I'm tired."

"It's okay. It's cute."

The compliment escapes me before I have time to think. The color of her cheeks spreads down her neck and my fingers pulse against her arm that I'm still stupidly touching. Her skin is soft beneath the pads of my fingers, and heat licks up my arm, moving through my body like wildfire.

Iris blinks slowly but neither of us look away. I've been an actor for a long time now, and I can confidently say I've never been this aware of someone. This locked in with them in such a short amount of time. Working with her so far, it's been as easy as breathing.

The scene today hasn't been very intimate yet, but it felt like it. It was as if I was using my character Hugh as a way to get to know her. The characters meet cute followed by the flirting and banter felt more like our own than Augie's incredible writing. Iris embodied the sweet yet bold nature of her character Juliette, and I don't think anyone on set could deny she's perfect for this role.

Every time we cut I could see the excitement and awe in Augie's eyes, and feel how pleased the rest of my pack was through the bond. Which I knew was also coming from the discovery that Iris was our Omega. A fact that's even harder to ignore when simply touching her arm and looking into her eyes feels like coming home. It's probably why it's so easy to slip into my accent with her. She feels safe.

"Iris, Jett, we're ready for you."

Iris inhales, her nose scrunching from the neutralizers. I'd planned to casually ask her why she wore them on our short lunch, but she'd run out with her assistant to her trailer claiming she needed to make a quick call.

She gently rubs her nose and breaks our connection, my arm dropping listlessly to my side. Her focus turns to Wilder and her shoulders pop back naturally when their eyes lock. It's not an uncommon reaction to him, his dominance oozes out of him without even trying, forcing people to pay attention. The man was born to be a Prime, and he's the best director I know. But for Iris, it's a bit different.

Omega's I've worked with aren't able to hold his eye contact for long. Their natural biological need to submit forces them to look away, but Iris, after our initial meeting and settling into herself on set, she holds his gaze firm, taking in every direction and note he's given her with confidence.

It's a turn on that she can hold her own, and her talent has floored me. I told Augie during lunch that as soon as we're off set, I want him to show me his favorite episodes of *Knot Hollows*, which he was both excited and smug about. Being a working actor, I hardly have time to watch anything, but I'll make time now. Weird? Maybe. But I want to see everything our Omega has done. Make up for the time I've missed with her.

"Let's do a quick rehearsal, then we'll shoot the wide shot," Wilder says.

"Sounds good," Iris replies.

"Jett?"

I pry my eyes away from our Omega to the face of my friend for twelve years and Prime. His brow is cocked, and there's a silent question in his eyes. He's been checking in with me relentlessly since my earlier outburst, one I apologized to Iris for multiple times. I couldn't exactly explain to her why my Alpha had freaked out, but thankfully she brushed it off and we started over.

"Sounds good," I say.

Wilder studies me a beat longer before stepping back. He offers his hand to Iris to help her down off her director's chair.

She's tall for an Omega, and capable of getting out of her chair by herself, but to my surprise she takes his hand. I don't think she realized she did it until she's standing, hand locked with his massive one.

The two of them stand in front of each other as if in a trance—the same trance I've felt every time I looked into her eyes today. My gaze drops to their joined hands, and it hits me this is the first time they've actually touched. And while Wilder's already accepted—at least as much as he can without her scent—what's obvious to me now, I can see his Alpha front and center. His hazel eyes have gone nearly black, his jaw flexing hard as he stares at her. The Prime is recognizing his Omega.

My own Alpha perks up, keeping watch over the situation. Wilder would never hurt her; he's got more control than any Alpha I've ever met, only rivaled by Mateo, but he's never touched his mate before—a mate I know he's longed for more than he's let on. I feel Mateo's presence and Augie's somewhere to my left, but I don't take my eyes off Wilder and Iris.

Our pack lead is 6'5", dwarfing her tall stature. His tattooed hand covers hers, the veins in his hand and forearm bulging from the grip he has on her. The two of them look good together, their dark hair and strong builds. He with his broad muscles and Iris with her soft curves. I've shared Omegas and Betas with him since college, and I can't stop myself from imagining what it would be like to share Iris with him. She'd look perfect, our knots stretching her pussy that was made to take us. To take our entire pack.

Blood flows south, my cock twitching in my jeans. Augie's pack bond perks up with calming energy and I blink, my gaze that had gone hazy with inappropriate thoughts snapping back into focus. Iris hasn't moved from her spot, her hand still locked in Wilder's grip. Her lips are parted slightly and Wilder's pupils no longer look like himself. They're completely dark, no hazel left. There's an intensity to them that nearly frightens me.

This is not good. First I nearly lose it to rage over a small bruise and now our always strong and level-headed Alpha is on the verge of rut? He thought that's what was happening to me, but no, Wilder is about to lose it.

Mateo appears next to our Prime with Augie, and my eyes meet their fearful ones. The crew around has stopped what they're doing and I swear you could hear a pin drop in this place. Thank fuck for NDAs and loyal crew because I have no doubt the weird shit that's been happening on this set today would be in the tabloids first thing tomorrow.

Omega, my Alpha growls. *Keep safe.*

Okay...well, that's not fucking good.

"Compa," Mateo speaks calmly. "Can you let go of Iris's hand?"

Wilder's low rumbling warning is his answer. He tugs Iris forward and she goes easily, her focus not leaving him. I observe her carefully, ready to yank her out of his grip if needed. But she doesn't appear afraid, her muscles loose and features relaxed.

"Omega," Wilder claims. His voice is lower than normal, his rough tone harsh and demanding.

"I am," Iris responds. Her voice isn't shaky, but at the same time I can tell it's not fully her—her Omega is speaking to her Alpha.

My heart rate speeds up and I look over to my packmates who are watching the exchange the same as I am. With shock, awe, but also worry.

Wilder tugs Iris the rest of the way into him, the action colliding her against his barreled chest. Fear lances through my gut as he dips his head to the smooth, unmarked column of her throat.

Despite being so close to them, there's no way we could stop him if he chose to sink his teeth into her. It wouldn't be an official mating bond since she has to be knotted and bite him back, but it would be a pack bond nonetheless and tie her to us without her consent. But thank the gods, he only drags his nose over her scent gland and inhales, his minty pheromones thickening around us.

"Jett," Mateo speaks softly.

I don't tear my gaze away from Wilder and Iris, but I hear Augie telling everyone we're wrapped for today and to leave.

"If he goes into rut, I'll get Iris out of here and you and Augie will stay here with Wilder," Mateo adds.

I know that's the best solution, even if my Alpha disagrees. Something else is happening here besides Wilder on the verge of rut, but I don't know what it is. We still haven't been able to scent her, and with the dose of rut blockers and the control Wilder normally has, this should not be happening.

Unless...

I don't have time to finish my thought, because the sweetest and neediest whine echoes through the set, followed by a pheromone cloud of saccharine strawberries. My brain short circuits as our Omega perfumes, burning through her de-scenters, and solidifying everything we already knew.

"Shit!" I hear Augie say through the haze of ripe-smelling fruit filling my senses. He's standing next to Mateo again, holding his mate's arm who's visibly reacting to her perfect scent, eyes wide and nostrils flared. My Alpha claws at my chest and mind, demanding me to cage Iris in with Wilder whose face is buried in her neck, inhaling her like a drug. Her hands are threaded in his hair, her nose pressed into his neck as well.

My own lemon pheromones burst out of me, mingling with hers and mixing with Mateo's honey, Wilder's peppermint, and Augie's mild basil. The perfect cocktail that I want our Omega to drink down.

There's no doubt about it; Iris Walker is our scent-matched Omega. Our mate.

My cock is rock hard and another whine curls through the air, this time with a pleading need. One only an Alpha can fill.

A purr builds in my chest along with my Alpha packmates, and another burst of bright strawberry perfume permeates the air alongside syrupy sweet arousal that can only mean she's producing slick.

"¡Maldita sea!" Mateo groans. "She's in heat."

Chapter Eight

Iris

Not good. This is not good.

It's great! My Omega preens as Wilder licks the column of my throat. Yes, licks. Slick gushes out of me, and there's no doubt in my mind my wardrobe is soaked. I'm lightheaded and I keep going in and out of being in control.

My Omega wants to run this show now. She's tired of being the understudy, waiting in the background to take the mainstage.

"Iris," a concerned yet soothing voice says near my ear. "Can you let go of Wilder?"

A deep and menacing growl vibrates through my being, the source of it from Wilder's chest, sending another wave of slick to my already soaked underwear. To any other designation standing within ten feet, that growl was a warning to back the fuck off, but to me, to my Omega, it was the sexiest thing we've ever heard.

There's cursing around me as I grip his silky dark hair tighter beneath my fingers, nostrils flaring, but all I smell is that damn scent neutralizer. I scrunch my nose and a pathetic whine pulls from my throat. I need a tissue so I can blow my nose. I need to smell him like he can so obviously smell me.

I press myself further into the massive Alpha whose body is nearly as heated as mine. We're like two stars burning bright in the galaxy, and his touch is setting me alight. His large palms drag down my curves to cup my ass, gliding my core against his massive dick, one that's hard and ready for me to ride.

Knot.

A pain rips through my stomach and I gasp. Had strong arms not been holding me up, I would have doubled over in pain. Fuck. It's been so long since I've had a heat—not to mention a heat around Alphas—I almost forgot how much it can hurt...*almost.*

My abdomen clenches again and I pull on the hair in my hands so hard Wilder grunts, his cock twitching.

"We need to get out of here," a soothing yet worried voice says. It sounds like Augie.

"We can't just take an unbonded Omega home with us, mi amor," Mateo answers.

"Then where? We have a nest."

"She hasn't consented," another growling voice replies with a southern twang, telling me it's Jett. "She's not in her right mind."

Annoyance claws at my chest that they're talking about me like I'm not here. I want to tell them off, tell them that while I may have knots on the brain, and feel like I'm burning alive from the inside out, I can consent. But the Alpha holding me to his chest begins to purr. The sound turns me into putty, the pain in my abdomen lessening and my rage easing.

"Little Omega," Wilder groans. "You smell so good."

My purr rattles to life in my chest. The sound is foreign, and I have no idea why I'm making it. Even the times I've gone to a heat clinic and had Alpha's help me through, I've never purred. Purring by an Omega is reserved for members of your bonded pack, soothing children, or...*mates.*

I told you, my Omega purrs. *They're ours.* Not just him. The whole pack.

An urgent need to scent him, to scent all of them, takes over, my Omega riding me to figure my shit out.

I dip my nose to where I know Wilder's scent gland is. But still all I get is the sterile scent of neutralizers. I whimper pathetically and bury my nose deeper against his throat. His hands grip me tighter and another touch soothes down my back in an attempt to comfort me, leaving a trail of pleasurable fire in its wake and more slick to produce from my very needy pussy.

"Easy, mi conejita."

Mateo. His hand is the one on my back, petting me so nicely. I never want him to stop. I inhale again against Wilder's neck and huff in frustration.

"Can you tell us what's wrong?" Mateo asks.

"The neutralizers," a wobbling female voice says. "She's going into heat and can't scent any of you."

A growl rips from my throat and I push away from Wilder. The movement is so fast and with strength I didn't even know I had, that he doesn't have time to pull me back.

I stalk toward the women who interrupted me, only stopping when two shaking hands are held in front of my snarling face.

"It's me, Iris! It's Sadie! I come in peace!" she squeaks.

"Get out!" Wilder growls at my back.

"No, I'm not leaving her," she contends, voice determined yet frightened.

Another person appears between us, my eyes now level with a lean chest. My narrowed gaze lifts to beautiful green eyes framed with thick-framed glasses.

"Iris." His voice is calm, like a soothing aloe to my heated skin. "Are you lucid enough to know who I am?"

"Augie," I say easily. My Omega may be at the surface, but I won't be completely lost to heat until it hits its peak. And now that I'm not held against Wilder and the other two Alpha's, I already feel a bit more clearheaded.

"Good," Augie murmurs. I hear some scuffling behind me and try to turn, but he takes my chin between his fingers so I can't look. Wilder growls and another one of the Alphas growls back. Pain lances through my low belly from the noise and I know I don't have much time before I'm on my knees and begging for a knot to ease me.

Fucking body betraying me. Fucking suppressants. I can't even smell Pack Quinn for fucksake and this is happening to me. Sometimes biology really is a bitch.

His thumb strokes my chin and I sigh at the calming feel of it. "You know who Sadie is right?"

My eyes dart behind him. Sadie peeks out, her eyes worried. Sadie. My assistant, a Beta. She's not here to take them from me. Right?

I blink a few times, my hormones leveling out the longer I'm not in Wilder's arms. My Omega isn't happy about that but I am. My head gets clearer the longer I stand here, and the longer I'm in Augie's calming presence, his touch gentle on my face.

"I do," I finally exhale.

"I need you to go with her, now," he says, keeping our gazes locked together.

"No!"

He doesn't blink at the outburst, his only reaction a small ghost of a sad smile. "We just gave Wilder an emergency rut blocker, but my pack is hanging on by a thread here."

Rejection washes over me and before I can stop myself my eyes fill with tears. Sadie cautiously steps beside Augie and I want to both hug her and snap at her. My Omega knows who she is but she doesn't like that she's here, her scent clear to the males in the room.

Augie drops his hand from my chin and I give my full attention to Sadie. She keeps her hands held up and voice low, eyes darting to the Alpha's behind me. I can't see them, can't smell them, and I'm not bonded to them, but I can feel their stress, their need for me. The air around us is like a rubber band about to snap.

"Iris," she says calmly. "I called the Omega clinic for you. They have a private room waiting, we just have to get you there."

No! Not that, please! my Omega pleads with me as an Alpha behind me growls.

The tears that had filled my eyes spill over my cheeks, and my nose runs. My gaze darts to Augie who looks pained, his square jaw clenched. He lifts his hand like he wants to wipe away my tears then stops. More tears spill and I reach up to wipe at my nose, having enough headspace to know I don't want to snot everywhere and embarrass myself more if that's even possible.

Sadie hands me a tissue she stashes in her purse in case of emergencies, and I note Augie's wide eyes the moment I bring it to my nose. His lips part but I don't hear what he says as I clear out my sinuses, the sterile smell of neutralizers leaving.

The moment the small rational part of my brain that was left realizes what I've done, my eyes widen too. My nostrils flare as multiple mouthwatering scents hit me.

Mint, lemon, honey, and the perfect hint of basil. My strawberry perfume bursts out of me, adding to the mix and creating what I can only describe as a cocktail meant to be the biggest aphrodisiac on the planet.

Ours. The Quinn Pack is ours. *Mine.* There's no denying it now.

Tears prick my eyes for a whole new reason and the desire to grab Augie and run into the arms of our Alpha's is tantalizing, but my feet stay glued to the spot, my mind still in shock at this revelation. One I never would have guessed to happen to me in a million years. Let alone on the set of my dream job, something I'll have to unpack later when biology isn't taking over and I'm feeling too many emotions mixed with needy arousal.

"Oh shit," Sadie mutters, realizing what she helped me do.

Oh shit is right. Heat flares through my body worse than before. Usually when I have a heat, especially after going off suppressants, I'll have pre-heat symptoms and a couple of heat spikes to warn me of what's to come, but this is different—a full blown first wave of heat. Once this is eased, they'll only get more intense until I'm completely lost to estrous.

I grip my abdomen and whine. Purrs erupt behind me and that doesn't do anything to help the situation.

"What do we do?" Sadie mutters. "Fuck, I fucked up."

"Iris," Augie grits out, his voice strained. "Can I touch you?"

I should say no, but there's no way I can't. I want his touch. *Need* his touch.

"Yes," I exhale, eyes watering from pain and need.

He grips my arms, his soothing touch easing me slightly. Enough I can look into his beautiful green eyes that remind me of his scent. Herbaceous basil, like it's been freshly cut. It's not as strong as mine or the Alpha's still at my back, but it's perfect, and I want to lick him to see how it tastes on my tongue.

"Do you feel it?" One of his hands leaves my biceps to tap over his heart.

I exhale through the pain in my body, focusing on the center of my chest. Where once it was just my heart beating, now there's an added sensation. A tug that pulls me toward him, like a string connecting us together. The more I focus, the more I feel that string pulling me to the Alpha's at my back, their purrs rattling in a way that makes it sound like they're in pain—restraining themselves from coming to me like our biology demands.

They need you, my Omega prods me. *Please!*

I swallow hard and nod.

"Good." He smiles, eyes shimmering with what look like tears. I don't know why that made him cry, but he doesn't look sad. Relieved maybe?

I take a breath in and his basil scent sparks further desire deep in my belly.

"Mi amor," Mateo growls. "Move faster, or get her out."

My Omega whines at what she thinks is rejection. Augie takes my chin in his and shakes his head. "No, beautiful. It's not what you think. We just don't want to take advantage."

"Please," I groan, even though I don't know what I'm pleading for.

"I need you to focus, okay?" His fingers pulse on my chin and I blink a few times to try and clear my mind.

I nod and he continues, "There are three very needy Alpha's behind you, and their biology is riding them hard to take care of you. To give you what you need, but we don't want to assume anything just because of this"—he taps his heart—"and your heat. So if you don't want their help, you have to go with Sadie now to the clinic."

A snarl bursts from my lips at the idea of being taken away from my scent matches. I could never let another pack touch me now, and to go through a heat alone with toys would harm me. Already my Omega feels as if she could be getting rejected. If I were to go through this heat alone, knowing that I found my scent-matched pack, it would ruin me.

"Do you not want me?" I ask, my voice more broken sounding and pathetic. But I can't find it in myself to care right now.

He looks confused for a moment before he cups my cheek, stroking his thumb over the heated skin. "I've wanted you for a long time, Iris. Even before I knew you were ours."

So many thoughts run through my head, so many questions. None of which I'm capable of asking right now. It's not like I've ever been in this situation before, nor did I ever plan to be. Finding your scent matches is rare, and going into heat like this doesn't happen much any more with all the medical advancements. But it's happening.

My stomach clenches in answer and I grit my teeth.

"If you want us to take care of you, we'll get you back to our place. We have a nest, it's never been used."

"You'll be there?" We may have just met, but I know my Omega needs him. It doesn't matter that he's a Beta, my Omega wants him. *I* want him to be there as ridiculous as that sounds. In some odd way, I feel like I've known him my whole life.

"If you want me to be, I will."

I nod vigorously and he smiles, the kind of smile that makes me want to throw my arms around him and kiss him.

"Does that mean you consent to Pack Quinn taking care of you through your heat, Iris?"

I nod but he shakes his head, holding my face firm in his hands now.

"I need you to use your words, sweet girl."

"Yes, I consent."

"If at any time you want to leave, you tell me and I'll get you to a clinic."

I know that won't happen, but I nod anyway, my Omega pushing hard against my mind to be set free completely and take over. She found her scent-matched pack, she's going into heat, she wants them, and I'd be a liar to say I didn't want them just as much, no matter how wild that sounds.

"August has my number," Sadie says. I flick my gaze to hers and she's not looking at me, but behind me. The scent of soothing mint invades my nose before the Alpha's presence is at my back.

"I'll contact you when I can, Sadie. Now go, we've got her, I promise," Augie says, his voice so strong in its conviction it would be impossible not to believe him.

Sadie gives me one last look and I do my best to nod and smile before she turns and hurries off set.

Before I can turn to meet the Alpha behind me, I double over, pulling away from Augie. Strong hands pick me up and my Omega already knows his touch and scent before I see his face. Wilder.

He holds me to him, hazel eyes no longer blown with near rut. They're still dark with desire, but there's something else in them. Awe maybe? Wonder?

"I've got you now, little Omega. It's going to be alright."

His deep voice rumbles against me, and in any other circumstance I'd think it was funny he was calling me little. But in his arms, I feel just that. His minty scent fills my nose and my purr springs to life again. He holds me closer and my body relaxes, feeling at ease in his arms.

"We finally found you," he whispers, and that's all it takes for me to pull his lips toward mine, and seal them with a kiss, not caring where we are or that I'm pretty sure my entire life and career has blown up in the matter of minutes.

A very big problem to worry about later.

Chapter Nine

Wilder

Mine, my Alpha chants. If there was any doubt at all before, there isn't any more. Her strawberry scent is perfect, made for me, for my pack, by the gods and goddesses themselves.

Her lips mold to mine, two puzzle pieces fitting together and locking into place. I was planning to wait to kiss her until we got somewhere safe, somewhere where the scent of others outside of our pack didn't irritate my Alpha, but I'm not going to complain about my Omega—my scent-matched Omega—being in my arms and kissing me.

Her purr inspires my own to resonate in my chest, sounding less rusty than it did before. Sparks buzz under my skin, and I'm grateful that Mateo and Jett were able to think quickly and get an emergency rut blocker into me. I've never felt that out of control like I did when Iris and I touched, but the moment our hands met, everything went to hell—or heaven considering she's the best thing I've ever tasted.

Sweet strawberry with a tangy undertone. I've always liked strawberries as a fruit, but now they will be my favorite. She's already my favorite treat in the world. I stroke my tongue against hers, savoring every note including an earthy nuance that's all hers, delving deeper into her mouth as she moans and perfumes, the air clouding with her pheromones and mixing with my own mint.

Iris's hands that are wrapped around the back of my neck squeeze me tighter. She's strong, a solid weight in my arms that

I never want to let go of. Her warm body writhes, a saccharine keening noise escaping from her throat and vibrating against my lips.

I open my mouth wider for her to explore, completely lost in every sensation swirling around inside me. I never thought I could feel so much so quickly for someone.

I never thought I could feel this much, ever.

Iris makes me and the dominant side that often scares people feel safe to come out. To fully step into my Alpha's sacred job as hers, her protector, the male that will help her feel so good.

My hand on her outer thigh grips her tighter, the pads of my fingers digging into the soft, warm flesh. Her tongue licks into my mouth and I faintly hear voices around us. I should growl, but I'm aware enough now to know it's my pack.

"Compa," Mateo's voice cuts through the strawberry fog clouding my mind. There's pressure on my shoulder and I hold in a warning snarl. He may be my packmate, but my Alpha wants to keep kissing his Omega. His mate.

"I know, but there's a car waiting to take us back to our place. Let's get out of here before we end up in a situation where we can't leave."

Before my lips can part from Iris, she pulls away first, her forehead dropping to my shoulder as she cries out in pain, fingernails digging into the back of my neck.

My purr intensifies in my chest to comfort her and another cloud of strawberry perfume permeates the air. Stifled moans from my pack join Iris's plight and my gaze meets Mateo's as he moves closer so he can place his hand on Iris's forehead that's shining with a light sheen of sweat.

"She's burning up." His eyes meet mine and I do everything in my power to fight my Alpha that so badly wants to lay Iris on the nearest surface, to plunge my cock deep inside her wet heat until every inch of my fat knot works itself inside her, stretching her wide and giving her what she needs—*what we both need*—now.

Jett appears at the other side of me, Augie to my front. Their focus is on the precious Omega in my arms. They're all barely holding it together as I am. The fact Augie is as on edge like the rest of us is further proof she's our mate. I didn't need any more proof, but only a scent-matched Omega could make a Beta look at an Omega like he is now—as if he's about to eat her alive.

"Alpha," Iris whines, her body attempting to fold in on itself in my arms. "Please Alpha, it hurts."

Her eyes are clamped shut tightly, her forehead wrinkled in pain. My purr swells and I hold her tighter into me.

"We know it does," Jett says before I can. "We're leaving now and we'll take care of you as soon as we get you to your nest."

She cries out painfully and I bellow, my Alpha not liking that Jett upset her, even if I don't know why his words would.

"Iris," Augie asks. "What is it, sweet girl? Can you tell us what upset you?"

I rumble my purr back to life. "Tell us, Omega."

She pries her watery eyes open, her silver-grey irises blown wide with lust and emotions. "I don't have a nest big enough for us."

Mateo and Jett's purrs join mine and I lean down to brush my lips against her forehead that's way too hot. "You do now."

Iris blinks, her pupils retracting a tiny bit. It tells me I'm looking at Iris now more than her Omega who's doing everything in her power to direct her.

"I'm sorry," she exhales, voice wobbly.

"There's nothing to be sorry for," I tell her.

She pushes at my chest and I reluctantly let her down, but keep my hand touching her low back. Her cheeks flush a deeper pink as she looks from me to the rest of my pack. I wish I could tell what she's thinking, what she's feeling. A bite would fix that right up and my teeth ache at the thought of claiming her—but that will have to come later—after her heat and after we've had time to court her. Even if I know she's our Omega, I'd never bond her until she gives me full permission outside of a heat and while I'm not holding back a rut.

Iris nibbles at her lower lip before she parts her mouth to speak. "I need you to know I didn't mean for this to happen."

"We know," I say. "But I'm glad it did."

"We all are," Jett says.

Her gaze moves from me, to Jett, to Mateo, and finally Augie, like she's trying to figure out what we're saying is true. Iris's Omega may know and accept we're hers, but just Iris is fighting it. Which is understandable. This isn't a normal situation or one any of us could have ever planned for. But what Iris will eventually understand, is I would give up everything for her. My job, our business, anything—and I don't even have to ask my pack if they feel the same. It's written all over their faces.

Her lips swollen from my kisses part but before she can utter another word, she doubles over, gripping her abdomen as the scent of her fresh slick grows thick in the air, nearly choking me.

Mateo bends over and takes her arm as I take the other; we try to help her stand straight but it's futile. Iris whines, her body going limp as she drops to her knees, body rocking forward like she wants to present for us right in the middle of this damn set.

"Fuck, I don't think we're making it out of here," Augie says the thought that had just come to my mind.

A low protest works its way up my throat, my Alpha refusing to accept that we're going to take care of our Omega through her heat on a set filled with our crew's scents.

I inhale a calming breath and get Mateo to help me pull Iris up. I grip her face in my hands as Mateo supports her from the back so she can't drop to her knees again and actually put that fine ass in the air. If she'd presented, no doubt every one of us minus Augie would have gone into rut. We may have torn each other to pieces just to fuck her first, and no one, not even our calming Beta, would have stopped us from doing it.

Alpha's may have evolved over the years and been able to use modern medicine to calm our instincts, but this hasn't been a normal situation and I feel how tight the pack bond is. We all love each other, but our scent-matched Omega in a surprise heat in a place that doesn't feel safe? We all are aching to claim her, to make sure no Alpha in a one-hundred-mile radius could take her from us.

"Omega," I grit out, my Alpha bark laced in my words.

She looks back into my eyes, pupils fully blown again.

"That's a good girl. I need you to listen to me, okay?"

She nods. "Yes, Alpha."

A burst of pheromones rushes through the room, not only mine but my packs. Hearing her say that pleased my hindbrain in ways I can't even explain.

"We need to get out of here and then we'll give you everything you need."

"Need," she exhales, the sound painful. "Need you now." She clenches her jaw.

"If one of us gives you what you need here, little Omega, I can't be sure we'll be able to leave. Don't you want a warm, safe nest?"

She tries to nod but then her eyes squeeze shut. "Alpha, please—"

"Give her what she wants, or I will," Jett growls. "I can't take seeing her in pain anymore."

I start to growl back but Augie's usually calm voice interjects, the sound of it near an Alpha's bark. "Oh for heaven's sake! I swear, you Alphas wouldn't survive without me."

I pry my gaze away from Iris as Augie moves to where there's a love seat near the fake bookshops front window. "Bring her here, she needs the edge taken off."

"Augie," Jett argues. "I don't—"

Augie growls, not an Alpha growl but one of warning. "Wilder and Jett, you go home and get the nest ready for her. Her heat will last for days and it needs to be comfortable for all of us. I will ease her for now, no dicks or knots, and Mateo will ride home with us in the car we have waiting."

The plan is logical, and while my Alpha wants to argue, I know it's for the best. I should be angry that Augie is thinking with a level head right now, but this is one of the many reasons Betas are imperative to pack life. They can be the voice of reason when biology takes over.

I brush my hand over Iris's cheek before leaning forward and scent marking her by rubbing my cheek over hers. A needy sound escapes her lips and I kiss them softly. "Did you hear what Augie said, Omega?"

She nods. "Do you think that will help you?"

"Yes, Alpha."

I look at Mateo and he dips his chin, pulling her from me. Jett hasn't said much to her yet but he comes forward and does the same, scent marking her so she'll have a piece of him while we leave her in the rest of our pack's hands.

Iris whines as she gets further away from us, but I hold myself back from going to her and place my hand on Jett's shoulder to stop him from doing the same. Augie's plan is a good one, and we'll be reunited with our Omega soon.

"Come on, let's go get our Omega's nest ready," I say to Jett as Iris settles on our Beta's lap.

Jett's blue eyes lock with mine and in them I see the same yearning I know is reflected in mine, but also an excitement.

We have an Omega—and hopefully, after her heat—we'll make our bond with her permanent.

Chapter Ten

August

I**F YOU HAD TOLD** me at any point in the last ten years that Iris Walker would be in my lap, in heat, and our pack's scent-matched Omega, I would have insisted that would only happen in my dreams.

Turns out, dreams do come true.

Her sweet strawberry perfume swirls in the air alongside Mateo's honey pheromones, making my mouth water and my dick painfully hard. Her dilated grey eyes that remind me of storm clouds, are zeroed in on mine, and her warm body rocks gently on my lap, knees bracketing my hips and her hands gripping my shoulders. Her body is so hot I'm surprised her clothes aren't damp with sweat.

I reach one hand up, keeping the other on her hip, and brush her dark hair behind her ear, my fingers trailing softly over her cheek. She shivers, oscillating her hips over my dick. The crotch of her jeans is damp with her slick, and if she wasn't in such need, and we weren't on set, I'd lay her out on the ground and eat her until all she knew was how to scream my name.

The love seat sinks next to me, and Mateo's honey scent gets stronger. Iris turns her face, her cheek resting in my palm as she looks at my mate—her mate now too. I can't believe I'm lucky enough to have found both of them. I can only hope that after the haze of her heat is over, she'll want to be ours like I know my pack already wants her to be.

"You're so beautiful, mi conejita," Mateo says.

Iris releases her bottom lip and smiles. "You are too." She flushes a deeper pink that makes her look similar to the delicious fruit she smells like, before she gives her gaze back to me. "So are you."

I blush now too, my cheeks becoming warm. I skim the pad of my thumb over her cheek, soaking in the fact Iris Walker, my crush for forever, called me beautiful, and she's mine.

Her hips rock with a bit more force, a small moan escaping from her plump lips as she chases the relief we promised her, her hot pussy dragging over my bulge before she drops her head forward, teasing her nose over my scent gland and marking me with her pheromones.

Fuck, that was hot. I drop my hand down to her ass, gripping both plush cheeks with my palms while lifting my legs a bit to give her more of the friction she's seeking.

Iris nips at my throat right over Mateo's mating bond scars and my dick jerks in my pants. If she does that again I'm going to come before she does, and that's not acceptable.

"Sweet girl," I groan, sliding a hand up her back and to the nape of her neck, gently coaxing her away from my throat.

Her hips grind into me at the same time she whines from the loss of my scent in her nose. Her heated gaze meets mine, her mouth in an adorable pout. Mateo chuckles when he sees it, his warm laugh vibrating through my body from where our arms touch. Iris glances over to our Alpha, my attention following hers.

Mateo's eyes are darker than normal, his scent mixing with another cloud of Iris's perfume, making the both of us groan. Mateo shifts on the couch, his erection evident through his jeans. Images of me and Iris sucking his cock at the same time flash behind my eyelids and Mateo's lip curls into a half-smirk, like he knew exactly what I was thinking. He probably does.

We're mates, and even though we can't communicate telepathically, I'm sure he felt the pulse of my desire down the bond. He also knows what I like, and I love sucking his thick cock while I jerk his fat knot. I know Iris will too, and I have no doubt she'll become addicted to his taste like I have.

"Do you need to come, Omega?" Mateo asks, his voice syrupy with his own arousal and desire.

"Yes, Alpha. Please," Iris beseeches, her hot pussy gyrating harder on my cock.

I hold her hips steady and grind my teeth together, her muscles flexing beneath my fingers as she tries to move. Fuck she's strong, but I'm stronger, keeping her in place.

"I need to move," she begs. "Please Augie."

Mateo twirls a strand of her dark hair around his finger, the color of it similar to his. Like a rich dark chocolate that's near black in color.

"What if our Beta touches that sweet pussy of yours, how about that, Iris?"

Goddamn. Our Beta. I really like the sound of that. The touching sounds really nice too. More than nice.

Her eyes widen and she nods vigorously. "Yes, I need—" Her words break into a whine and by the way she attempts to fold in on herself, I know it's another cramp.

Sweat breaks out on my forehead from the arousal in my body, Iris's hot curves against me, and the bright light of the set that still shines down on us. I'm never going to be able to look at this bookstore again in the same way.

"Do you trust me, mi conejita?" Mateo asks.

"Yes," she says without having to think about it, and Mateo purrs in delight. The best thing an Omega or mate can do is say they trust their Alpha. It's an immediate aphrodisiac.

Mateo tugs Iris to him, pulling her from my lap so her top half is laying over his thighs and her legs now drape over mine. She squeaks as he maneuvers her easily, his muscles flexing as he props her head up on one of the cream pillows and makes sure she's comfortable.

Her creamy skin pinkens, throat turning a splotchy red, but her Omega is fighting to stay in the driver's seat, her thighs falling open so Mateo and I can see the mess she's made of her jeans.

"Pull down her pants, mi amor. I want to see you play with her pretty pink pussy. Let's see if she tastes as good as she smells."

My cock thickens and pulses, my mouth watering. I hadn't planned to eat her out here—that felt like it would just remain a fantasy—but Mateo has given me an order, his Alpha has taken over, and I'm not going to say no. I had the set secured, and nobody is going to walk in here.

I shift on the loveseat that's too damn small for this, but thankfully I'm fairly flexible. Mateo and his deft fingers undoes our Omega's jean button, lowering the teeth of the zipper for me, while holding her on his legs with his other hand. Her chest rises and falls in short breaths, her hips wiggling in anticipation. I know she needs to be eased, we've made her wait long enough, and I'm thirsting for a taste of her pussy, but I absorb this moment.

Iris Walker, my dream girl, our scent-matched Omega, being held for me by my mate, my Alpha, while on the set of a film I wrote. We're going to be very behind schedule now, but I couldn't care less. I'll fund the whole goddamn movie if the investors pull out, or we don't even have to shoot it ever. If today only served to bring her into our lives, that's fine with me. Because I know this was meant to happen.

I smile roguishly at her, removing her shoes before pushing my glasses up my nose. I lean forward, inhaling her sweet, heady scent, hooking my fingers into the loops of her jeans. I pause briefly and hold her eye contact; she nods her permission and I drag the coarse fabric down over the generous curves of her hips until the V between her thighs is revealed, her sex covered in a soaked pair of white cotton underwear.

The scent of her arousal invades all my senses, and it's like we're in the middle of a ready-to-pick strawberry field. If my mouth wasn't closed I'd be drooling. I lift my gaze to Mateo to see how he's fairing.

His grip on Iris is strong, fingers indenting the flesh of her outer arm, while his other holds her hand nearest to him tightly. I have no doubt his cock is pressing into her back, and I admire my mate's strength. Between Jett's alpha-rage and Wilder's almost rut, I nearly expected him to join them in a similar biological reaction. But while his neck is tight with restraint, and his nostrils are flared taking in her scent, he's handling himself well.

I shouldn't be surprised. He's always been able to control his Alpha in a way many of his designations cannot. He claims it's years of mind/body practices like yoga, meditation, running, and weight lifting, but it's more than that.

My mate is a master at edging. Not only with his own desire but with mine. He loves to make me go without taking my pleasure when I've been naughty, and he likes to test the limits of his own denial as well. He's a giver by nature like I am, but he thrives on how it feels to go without coming for long periods of time so the payoff is greater. In a way, Iris in heat is his ultimate test of restraint, and so far he's passing. Even if this is the most on edge I've seen him, he's still holding himself together.

Iris wiggles her hips and I draw my attention back down her body. I could tease her, take my time pulling her pants off and kissing up every inch of her skin, but that will have to wait for another day. She's already waited long enough, and I don't want to test my patience any longer either.

I drop her pants beside us and hook my fingers in the band of her underwear. Her body is warm under my touch, nearly too warm. It makes me feel even worse for not easing her sooner, so I waste no time in shucking them down, tucking the soaked fabric into my pocket. I'm keeping these as a souvenir; maybe I'll tease my Alpha's with them, or use them to get Mateo off later. My dick jerks and I know that's exactly what I'm going to use them for.

"Look at you, sweet girl," I mutter as I take in Iris's half-clothed body. I place my palms on the outside of her legs and drag them up, pushing open her thighs further to make room for my body.

Iris moans at my touch, hips lifting toward my face as I wrap her legs around me. Her pussy, the mound of it curved with neatly trimmed dark hair is perfect. Her slit is pink, lips wet and gleaming, slick already leaking down to coat her inner thighs. Mateo is muttering to our Omega in Spanish, "Dioses. Eres perfecta, Omega. Tan madura y fragante." *Gods. You are perfect, Omega. So ripe and sweet smelling.*

I inhale her like one would a candle and agree with my mate. I haven't even tasted her yet, but I know I could eat her out every day. I want to walk around smelling like her and Mateo, let the entire world know who I belong to.

"Keep your legs around me, Omega," I command. It's not a bark since I'm not an Alpha, but Mateo's eyes widen in amusement at the hard tone of it. I smirk at Iris. "I'm going to make you feel so good, okay?"

She nods vigorously and I move my hands to spread her pussy open with my thumbs, the swollen skin deep pink with need and slick beneath my touch. Her clit pulses and I swipe my thumb over it. She jackknifes upward, pussy nearly touching my lips. Mateo shushes her, holding her so she can keep her balance.

"Yes!" she cries. "I need more."

I rub my thumb back the other way and then in circles. She keens, pressing up again for more sensation. If this were Wilder or Mateo between her thighs, I'd have no doubt they'd smack her pretty pussy and demand she wait like a good Omega for the pleasure they give her, but lucky for her, I'm not them.

She moans when I add pressure, legs gripping around my body to try to draw me in closer, no doubt wanting my mouth on her. But I'm not done playing yet.

I lick my lips and glance up at Mateo. He's watching Iris carefully, a wolfish smile on his beautiful lips. "You like your Beta's fingers on you, mi conejita?"

I see that nickname is going to stick even though the neutralizers in her nose are long gone. It suits her, though, and I foresee lots of fun play coming in the form of plugs fashioned as bunny tails and of course ears.

My mate loves toys, as she'll probably find out. So does Jett, I've seen his collection he thinks is a secret only Wilder knows about. The guy has an entire chest full of stuff the two of them use on their partners. But, they're going to have to get all new stuff now that we have an Omega of our own. One that deserves to have things that are her and our packs alone. Just like the nest that's gone unused in our home.

Iris whines, though this whine is one of desire instead of pain. "Yes, I like them."

I increase the pressure of my thumb, dragging my other hand through her wet slit until I'm at her entrance. I slide two fingers in, her walls fluttering around me, her tight Omega pussy greedy for a knot. I can't give her that, but I'm good with my mouth and fingers. At some point during her heat I hope I'll be able to use my fist as a knot—something I've done before and enjoy doing.

Our Omega.

Those two words inspire me to make her feel the best she's ever felt, give her the best head she's ever had. I push my fingers in deeper until they can't go any further, hooking them forward when I find her G-spot at the same time I press my thumb over her clit.

Iris shouts my name and slick flows from her pussy down my wrist, her body trembling as it barrels toward release. I want her to come, but not until I've tasted her. I let up on her G-spot, removing my thumb but holding her open. Mateo speaks softly to her, his eyes meeting mine right before I seal my lips over her clit.

Her flavor bursts across my tongue, the strawberry flavor of her so delicate and ambrosial—I've never tasted anything quite like her. Mateo's cum is sweet too, but with a masculine undertone I can't quite describe, where Iris is all feminine perfection, with floral undertones.

I lap around her clit, sucking and tasting, slowly drawing my fingers in and out of her pussy. Her inner walls attempt to clamp down, searching for a cock and an Alpha knot. The movement only makes me want to fuck her faster, provide her at least a bit of relief even if it's not by my dick.

I slide a third finger in and she cries out, her free hand not in Mateo's flying down to grip my hair, pulling it tight in her fingers so my scalp stings. She presses me into her pussy and I hear our Alpha chuckle.

"She's trying to ride your face, mi amor. It's sexy as hell."

I moan around her clit, agreeing with him. I become a man obsessed with getting her off. Licking up and swirling my tongue over the pulsing bundle of nerves.

"Are you going to come, Omega?" Mateo purrs, a darkness under his tone that's all dominant Alpha. My dick throbs at the sound of it.

"Yes!" she cries, hand pushing me harder between her thighs.

I hear the sound of kissing and for a moment I wish I could look up and witness Mateo and Iris's first kiss, but I have a job to do, and I feel how close she is to coming. Her body shakes, thighs trembling, and pussy milking my fingers as I thrust them deeper and harder, hitting her G-spot with each stroke.

I take her clit between my lips and give her one last hard suck, pressing my fingers firm against the rough patch of skin inside her.

"Augie!" she screams, hips thrusting into my mouth as she does exactly what I'd hoped, squirting all over my hand and couch, berry-scented perfume flooding around us. My dick jerks in my pants as I come, having not even been touched. I should be embarrassed but I'm not. Giving her pleasure and the taste of her alone set me off.

I lap up all her sweet juices, not wanting to waste a drop, working her through her orgasm as her fingers pulse against my scalp. When she finally releases me, I look up from between her still quivering thighs, my mouth wet and lips swollen. Mateo's lips are red too, a bit of what was left of Iris's lipstick having transferred to his mouth. He looks hot as hell and I'd love to kiss him, but I know we need to leave like we'd planned before Iris needs us again.

I gently sit up, sliding my fingers from her sated pussy and using the back of my wrist to push up my glasses that have slightly fogged up. Iris observes me with hooded eyes, pupils clearer than before and her breathing more even. I bring my fingers to my lips but Mateo reaches out and stops me.

"Bad boy," he tsks. "You don't get to be greedy with our Omega's cum."

Iris's heated gaze is on us as Mateo pulls my hand to his lips, sucking my slick coated fingers into his mouth. His hot tongue licks every drop, swirling over my digits as if he's sucking my cock. Said spent dick fills with blood once more, but before I can tell him to stop before things get heated again, he pulls back and purrs, eyes dropping down to the Omega still laying over his lap, head propped up on the pillow and skin flushed.

"Best pussy I've ever tasted."

Iris's purr springs to life and Mateo looks down upon her adoringly. Her cheeks pinken from his stare, eyelids fluttering shyly.

Her lucidity reminds me it's time to leave. I don't know how much time we'll have before another wave of heat takes over, one that I have no doubt will be stronger, and our pack is waiting for us.

"Iris." I draw her attention to me. "How are you feeling?"

She inhales and attempts to sit up. Mateo helps her but doesn't let her pull away from him. I expect her to try to get away again but instead she relaxes into his hold, eyes still on mine.

"I'm feeling better now, thank you. Just tired."

Mateo brings the back of his hand to her forehead and hums. "Your fever is better right now, but we should go. You can sleep in the car on the way to our home and your nest."

Her brow furrows, unsure emotions fluttering across her features.

"I know this is all a lot, Iris," Mateo says. "And now that your head is a bit clearer you're thinking more about what all this means. But please, let us take you home and help you through the rest of your heat. We'll all be good to you, I promise." He grips her hands in his and kisses her knuckles.

Iris holds his gaze, and I swear I can hear her thinking and debating on her next move. Eventually, and to my relief, she nods. Mateo's relief pulses through our bond as well, and my shoulders I didn't realize had gone tense relax. Had she said no, we would have done whatever she asked of us, but I'm glad we don't have to worry about that.

"Let's go," she yawns, pulling out of Mateo's grasp. It's then she realizes she's still naked from the waist down. She nibbles on her lower lip before looking at her pants on the set floor then to me. "But I'm going to need a new pair of pants first."

Me too.

Chapter Eleven

Iris

My pussy tingles from the pleasure Augie gave me—the best pussy eating I've ever had in my life. The hot Beta that smells like freshly plucked basil was practically making out with it, and I'm not complaining. His rough tongue felt delicious against my throbbing clit. Then there was Mateo...

His dominating kisses, soothing voice, and the way his strong body held me through my pleasure. He smells and tastes like freshly harvested honey, but not in an overwhelming way. Like just the right amount you'd stir into your tea. My mouth waters as my Omega agrees with me, and a brief cramp ripples through my low abdomen.

I take a slow inhale so the honey and basil scents swirling with mine don't overwhelm me. It's futile considering I'm in the back of an SUV with Mateo and Augie, an older bonded Beta driver behind a partition in the front who I thankfully can't smell nor can he smell us. It would be embarrassing if he could.

Slick that won't stop leaking out of my pussy floods the air and I'm even more glad now that there had been a rack of clothes wardrobe rolled in with an identical pair of jeans I'd been wearing before. But, I have no underwear on, so I know by the time I reach Pack Quinn's home, they'll likely be ruined. It would help if I had underwear, but I couldn't find them. Granted, those were soaked too.

I squeeze my eyes shut and exhale the breath I'd pulled in. I'd hoped to fall asleep in the car, but after my orgasm my head became clearer and my brain won't shut up. Neither will my Omega. I can't stop thinking, wondering if agreeing to the pack helping me was the right idea.

It is. They're ours. Our mates.

They are. That much is true. It's hard to deny when they smell like heaven to me. When simply being around them threw me into heat even after a year of suppressants, and the scent neutralizer up my nose. I should have known something was different before even going on set, given I was already feeling on edge. It's like my instincts knew who Pack Quinn would be to me before I even met them.

Mint, lemon, honey, and basil—perfect compliments to my strawberry scent. My mouth waters again just thinking about what they'd all taste like together. Images of me on my knees, four males above me, their cocks out as I open my waiting mouth to be fed floods my mind. My mates giving me what my Omega body so desperately needs and craves—has craved for a long time, yet I've done everything in my power to deny myself of it.

And look where it led me. Yes, I've found my scent matches, but I've ruined the movie and potentially my career. Nobody will want to hire me when it's found out I went into heat on set. Gods, I shouldn't have even been there in the first place. I told them I was on suppressants; it was in my contract that I was. I know the scent match made things worse for me, and I couldn't have predicted that, but would I get in trouble with their insurance? Or their investors?

Regardless of what happens, this could mean the end of my acting career. The career I've not only worked hard to have but sacrificed so much for. Even my health and basic biological needs. Every pleasure I felt from my mind-blowing orgasm Augie gave me, and the kisses with Wilder and Mateo, Jett's touch, go out the window.

I grit my teeth as a feeble whine builds in my throat. I may have been eased through the first wave of my heat, but that was just the beginning. When I'm fully in the midst of my cycle, I'll be lost to the haze of knots, pleasure, and breeding. Thank gods I'm on the birth control shot, a fact I'll have to tell the pack before we're intimate again. There's a lot I should tell them before then, but I don't want to speak right now in fear my hormones will take over and I'll just cry.

My skin itches, and I want to reach out to the bonded Alpha and Beta pair for comfort. We're on a bucket seat in the back of the SUV, Augie next to me and Mateo on the other side of him.

Before I closed my eyes they were holding hands, and I can't help but wish I'd let Augie hold mine too. He offered but I shook my head no, thinking it was better to not touch during the enclosed car ride, one they said should take under thirty minutes this late at night—or early in the morning depending on how you look at it since it's after two in the morning.

Ugh, this is such a mess. I'm a mess. A touch starved, reckless, mess, who ruined their film. I was supposed to be the solution to their problems, and now I've made an even bigger one. I should have never taken this job.

My Omega doesn't like the idea of having done that and not having met her mates, because a cry sneaks out of me before I can stop it, the bridge of my nose stinging with the warning of tears.

"Iris?" Mateo asks, his voice laced with concern. "What is it?"

I don't open my eyes and I don't dare to answer him. If I do either, I'll lose it. What will they think of me then? They just helped me through a wave of heat and are taking me home to help me through the rest of it; I don't want them to think I'm not grateful. But I wonder if I wasn't their scent match, what would have happened then?

A tear leaks out of my still closed eyes and I scrunch my nose to keep it from running. I feel Augie move beside me and some noises; it isn't until the scent of honey fills my nose I know the

Alpha and Beta have switched places. He doesn't touch me but his purr springs to life and the weight of the seat dips next to me as he sits.

"Mi conejita," he rumbles. "Your silence and tears are killing me. Please look at me and tell me what's wrong so I can fix it."

There's a tentative touch against my cheek, turning my face to his. It's light, waiting for further invitation to continue. I should pull away, but I can't. Not only is Mateo one of my scent matches, but I'm an Omega in heat. A touch starved one at that. His warm skin feels too good, and his purr is already relaxing me.

I let my cheek fall into his palm before I finally open my eyes. It's dark in the cab of the car, but with the lights of L.A. outside the windows, I see his concern written on his features. I imagine his Alpha is riding him hard like my Omega is. I'm in distress and he needs to comfort me.

"*Please.*"

"Please what, Omega?"

I swallow, realizing I said the word out loud. I think I'm getting closer to another wave of my heat. My Omega is pushing at me to take over again, to let this handsome and caring Alpha take care of us. I want him to, but not yet. I need to let them know what kind of Omega they're dealing with here. That this heat is going to be far from normal. But I should tell their pack all together.

I blow out a breath and collect myself as best I can, bringing my hand up to grip Mateo's wrist. He smiles softly at my touch, his purr growing louder. My muscles relax despite my thoughts, and my speeding heart rate slows.

"I need to tell you something," I say.

Mateo's thumb strokes my cheek, his features remaining calm despite the anxiety-inducing phrase I just spewed.

"Anything, Omega. What is it?"

I shake my head slightly. "How long till we reach your place?"

The movement of his thumb doesn't stop. "We're nearly there. Five minutes tops."

Only five minutes till we get to their place, then a little bit longer for me to tell them everything and maybe exchange some pleasantries before they feed me their cum and fill me with their cocks and knots for the next three to five business days.

I shake that off and think about what I would even want to know about them beyond what I've read in entertainment magazines. The idea of asking them what their favorite color is before they fuck me across the mattress is ridiculous and I laugh at myself for thinking it.

Mateo smiles back, his roguish grin visible even in low light. It sets my fucking perfume off like a bomb. I hear his groan of desire before his thumb on my cheek stills and his hand tenses. Not good.

Yes, good, my Omega insists. But she's clearly a confused hussy, because I'm trying to keep sex from happening in the back of this SUV, and now that I've thought about it, I would like to know something personal about the men I'm going to fuck.

Mateo and I lock eyes again, and I'm glad he's still holding my cheek because I have the biggest urge to look down and see if he's hard. I have no doubt he is, and I'd be a liar if I said I haven't thought about what his cock will look like and feel like inside me ever since I felt the heat of it pressing into my back while he held me and Augie ate me like his last meal.

"What do you need to tell me?"

His words bring me back to the present. "I—" Pain ripples through my abdomen, cutting off my words. Fuck. I don't know if I'm going to make it five more minutes let alone longer than that, especially when I'm surrounded by their entire pack instead of just two of them.

Mateo's seductive honey scent strengthens in my nose, and I greedily inhale like it's a drug. That was stupid of me, because a gush of slick produces between my thighs.

His purr turns to more of a throaty growl, and much like his moan, it doesn't help the situation between my thighs. My core throbs and I clench my legs together as another cramp ripples through me. Fuck, this heat wave is coming on fast and I can't stop it. The orgasm before helped to curb my need but I don't just need to come, I need a knot.

"Mateo." I reach out frantically for his free hand and grip it.

"What's wrong? What do you need?" His voice is slightly panicked and for a brief moment I feel bad for making him anxious.

"What's your favorite color?"

The SUV goes quiet before both him and Augie bark a singular laugh. I realize it's funny, but I'm being serious.

Mateo sees that I'm not laughing and swallows before answering, "Yellow."

My lip tilts at the corner. Yellow makes sense. He reminds me of sunshine, and his skin is warm like it too. I imagine laying on a blanket in the park with him, the California sun shining on us, and his honey taste on my tongue as we kiss—it makes me both happy and sad. The image is lovely, but we aren't going to be basking in the sun together during my heat, and I don't know what will happen between us after it's over.

I push that thought away before my Omega can dwell and I start crying again. "What about you, Augie?"

I pry my gaze away from Mateo, his hand dropping from my cheek as I look at the Beta seated on the other side of him.

"Grey," he says easily.

I raise an eyebrow. "Grey?"

He pushes his glasses up the bridge of his nose like he did after he ate me out, lips wet from my cum. It was hot and adorable at the same time, two things I didn't know could coincide. "I should say silver." He clears his throat. "Like the color of your eyes."

The heat that's been building down below spreads upward, my skin turning into fire. I shift in my seat, the clothes on my body way too itchy. My hands grip the bottom of the shirt I have on and I pull at it, hating the way it feels on my skin. I want soft blankets that feel like butter. I want a nest that smells like my pack—well, not my pack yet. We're not even going to my nest since it wouldn't be big enough.

Frustration scratches at the back of my throat. I hate that I don't know what this one looks like. Mateo and Augie assured me no other Omega has been in it, but while my Omega is happy to be taken care of by her scent matches, and that we're going to go through a heat with them, our biology craves familiarity and comfort. I don't like not knowing what it's going to be like, or how the room is going to feel.

I whine and instead of turning away from Mateo like I tell myself to, I nearly dive into his lap. The only reason I don't fully do so is because the seat belt I'm wearing prevents me from it, so my face ends up near his armpit.

Alpha, my Omega purrs. "Help."

"We're pulling into our driveway. We'll help you when we're inside."

I stifle an embarrassed groan. I didn't mean to say help out loud, but I do need help. The pain is growing unbearable, and my pheromones are so strong now, the only reason I smell Mateo is because my nose is directly near a scent gland.

He rubs my arm just as the car jerks, coming to a complete stop.

"Can you walk, Iris?" Augie asks.

My Omega grumbles no at the same time I say yes—two competing answers. But I'm not an invalid; I can get in the house by myself. I pull my nose away from him and sit back. He unbuckles my seatbelt before I can, his arm and hand brushing against me. I bite my lip when my clit pulses and nearly jump him and beg for his knot. Thankfully the car door opens beside me and cool night air filters into the cab.

The change of scent and intrusion both is a relief and an annoyance. My Omega liked the smells of us, but without them a bit of the pain ebbs, enough I should be able to walk safely to their home before anything embarrassing can happen in front of the driver. I'm still trying to forget I fell to my knees and nearly presented myself in front of all of them earlier.

Before I can make my way out of the car Mateo stops me with his hand on my thigh. The pressure feels good on my body and I want to ask him to move it closer to my pussy, but I don't. I look up into his eyes and find him smiling.

"You didn't tell us your favorite color."

I smile back at him. "Purple."

Mateo's eyes widen just enough that I notice. "I'm really glad to hear that."

Before I can ask him why, the scent of lemons hits my nose followed by the soothing smell of mint. I perfume and double over in my seat, my inner walls clenching around nothing.

Alphas. Our Alphas.

"Yes, they're yours. We're yours, Iris. All of us," Mateo says with such conviction I want to believe him. Also, shit, I said that out loud too. My Omega is clearly back in charge now.

My thoughts jumble as Mateo ushers me from the car, his hand on my back. Jett's hand takes mine as I step to the ground, and I meet his ocean blue gaze that's darker in the late evening. There's muted speaking I can't hear going on behind me, but with Jett holding my hand and Mateo at my back with his hand on my hip, I don't care what's being said or not said.

A thought I have to tell them tries to push through the haze of heat that's taking over, but I can't remember what I needed to tell them. All their scents, the presence of their pack surrounding me again, it's too much and also not enough.

I double over and grip my stomach, but before I can do anything else I'm being lifted, this time by Jett.

I bury my nose against his neck and inhale the lemon scent that smells almost like lemon bars straight from the source. I lick his neck, tangy sweetness sparking on my tongue, and Jett groans, muscles flexing around me as he holds me tighter.

"Don't do that, Omega, or I'll fuck you right here on the ground."

"Okay," I reply, licking him again so he shudders.

There's a warm chorus of male laughter but all it does is make me wetter. The sounds zapping electricity to my already pulsing clit. We move up the steps and someone must open the front door because light filters in. I wince, not liking it. Omegas crave the darkness and comfort of their nests during heat or times of distress, and being in the foyer of a house that's lit with artificial light after the darkness of the car doesn't make me happy.

"Shhhh, my star, I'm taking you to your nest."

My star. I don't know why he called me that, but my Omega likes it. I like it. I suck over Jett's scent gland in thanks and my perfume curls around us. My belly clenches at the same time I finally remember part of what I wanted to tell them.

"Touch starved," I say, clinging to him harder.

Jett doesn't balk; he continues walking, carrying me like I weigh fifty pounds instead of two-fifty, his purr kicking to life and wrapping around me like a heated blanket, soothing me.

"It's okay," he hums. "You won't be for much longer."

Arousal curls like smoke in my stomach, rising up until I swear my entire body is vibrating with it. I bury my face in his neck, dragging a long lemony inhale as a door is kicked open and I pry my head up to look at the room we just walked into.

Holy dream nest.

It's stunning and decorated in every beautiful shade of purple you could imagine. Now I understand Mateo's reaction to my favorite color. If I was more in my right mind, I'd make a joke about them stalking me, but I know they haven't.

I try to get down from Jett's arms so I can fully take it in, but pain and heat explodes through me and I whine, my body curling into itself as my Omega takes over, demanding her needs finally be met after so long.

"Knot," I cry, against Jett's chest. "Please, Alpha. Give me your knot."

Chapter Twelve

Jett

"I thought you took the edge off!" Wilder growls from behind me as I hold Iris to my chest, moving to the edge of the oversized round bed in the corner of her nest.

"We did," Mateo growls back. "Now calm down or get out. An Omega's nest needs to be peaceful, not full of Alpha bullshit."

He's right about that. But I feel for Wilder. I know that if I didn't have my Omega mate in my arms, I'd probably feel the same as him. Our instincts are riding us hard, and leaving her on set, in heat, in need, was not easy for us, even though it had to be done. The housekeepers we have come once a week have kept the nest and Omega suite in our home clean, but it's never been used. It was devoid of scents, and while I've never tended to Iris during her heat, I know what she needs.

Omegas need the scents of the pack in their nest. If we had Iris leading up to now, she would have been nesting for at least a week before, most likely stealing our worn clothes and weaving them into her safe space. Since that couldn't happen, Wilder and I went through the house and dug through laundry hampers, pulling out items that smelled like each of us. I didn't dare weave them in the nest, but we've left them in a pile on the bed for her.

In my mind, I saw them pulling up in the car, Iris being shown the nest, and getting to watch her smell each item and build the haven we'll spend the next few days in, but that isn't going to happen. At least not yet. Not that I'm complaining. My Omega is in my arms and begging for me to take care of her, so I'm going to do just that.

I'm aware of Wilder and Mateo speaking to each other in hushed tones, but I tune them out. Augie appears next to me just as Iris licks right over my scent gland, her nails digging into the back of my neck as I try to put her down on the bed. My cock swells against the placket of my jeans, throbbing with the need to be inside her. To knot her until she's satisfied and sleeping in my arms.

"Shhh, Omega." I grip her tighter to me when she whines, purring for her deep enough that her body vibrates from the strength of it. "I'm going to give you what you need, but I need to put you down so I can do that. Alright?"

It takes a second for my words to register, but a moment later she relaxes her hold on me enough that I can gently lay her on the bed, her pale skin and long dark hair a beautiful contrast on the dark purple sheets. Later I'll take the time to study her body, memorize the curves and lines of it like a script, but now isn't the time for languid kisses and explorations. She said she was touch starved, that she needs my knot, and I'm done holding back.

Iris reaches for me, but before I ask for permission to enter her nest and finally kiss her, Augie stops me with a hand on my chest. My gaze flashes to him and I hold in a growl. My Alpha doesn't like that he's stopping me from claiming my Omega—*I* don't like it.

He holds up his other hand in surrender. "I know, Jett. I know, but I had planned to ask her if she was on any form of birth control, and we need to know before this goes further."

My dick twitches and if Augie's soothing Beta energy wasn't pumping through our bond. I think I may have snapped into a rut at the image of making a baby with the beautiful Omega begging for me.

Heats are designed for breeding. Days of nothing but knots and filling your Omega up with cum to get them pregnant. I'd love a family, but our pack hasn't talked about children much. We did when we originally formed, but it hasn't come up since. Not that there would have been a reason to since we weren't actively seeking an Omega and work takes most of our time.

Iris perfumes, and I inhale deeply, her strawberry pheromones overtaking my senses. She can't know what I'm thinking, but by her scent, her Omega heard Augie and thought about it too. She no doubt loves the idea of getting pregnant, it's ingrained in our biology, but I don't think Iris outside of her heat haze would like that. She just met our pack, and we haven't even courted. Everything is being clouded by our scent match and her heat. Her Omega is trying to run the show and my Alpha is right there, pushing at me to fuck her hard and fast, come deep inside her womb and knot her so not a drop of my cum can escape her pussy.

Iris reaches out to me again, her face both pained and eyes dejected. I grit my teeth and push against Augie's hand still on my chest. He continues to hold me back and I look away from Iris's worried eyes. "I'll find out, don't worry, Augie. I won't do anything she doesn't want, you know I won't."

He stares at me a beat before he finally exhales, shoulders dropping in resignation. I may be on the brink of a rut this time instead of rage; I don't think any Alpha wouldn't be this close to their scent-matched mate in heat, but I'd never do anything she didn't want, nobody in our pack would or could.

Iris whimpers and the sound lances through my heart as if I'm being stabbed. "I'm going to lay down with her now, and you can join us if you'd like," I tell our Beta.

He looks relieved, and even though I want to be knot deep in Iris already, I'm glad he stopped me and we had this moment. I knew a pack once where their Beta doesn't take part in heats because they don't have a knot, but that's not how our pack works, or I work. Augie is a part of us, and he's Mateo's mate;

he'll be here alongside us every step of the way. Especially since Iris wants him here.

I don't know what happened between them on set after we left, but he smells heavily of her arousal. I have no doubt he was the one who eased her, because if Mateo had knotted her they would have had this conversation already, and they would have not gotten here so quickly. Alpha knots go down faster in a heat, but not that fast.

My cock kicks up at the idea that I'll be the first one to knot her. I have no doubt if Wilder was more of a cocky asshole, he'd be the first since he's the Prime of our pack, but that's not how he is. He may be the most dominant, but he knows Iris is running the show here, and if my star wants me, then I'm going to give everything to her and more.

I quickly undo my shirt and throw it to the side of the bed. Iris observes me with wide eyes, licking her lips as her gaze trails over my abs and across the tattoos on my chest, different ones I've collected over the years including the black and grey ouroboros I have on my right bicep that matches the rest of my packs.

"Can we come into your nest, sweet Omega?" I purr.

Gratitude from my pack comes through the bond at my question, happy that I included all of us and not only me. It's always good to get permission to enter an Omega's nest, even if it's clear they want you in it. It shows respect and sets the tone for the rest of their heat.

"Yes, please," Iris moans, thighs clenching together in need.

I don't wait longer; I bend over her and place my hands on either side of her head. Her fingers glide up my ribcage, her heated touch creating a wave of arousal through every nerve and synapse. I shiver, her hips arching up so her sex rubs against my bulge, the friction delicious.

Her hands slide up to my shoulders and attempt to pull me down flat on top of her but I tsk. "Not yet, star." I brush my mouth over hers to stop the objection already leaking from her parted lips. "I need you to focus."

She tries to pull my body down again and I chuckle. Our Omega may be smaller than me and my pack, but she isn't weak.

I move back enough that I can stare into her eyes. She's pouting, thrusting her hips up again in search of my cock. I smirk, letting her seek me out but not giving her what she wants.

"Iris, I have an important question to ask you." I lace my voice with a bite of a bark so she stops her motions, pupils retracting. Her chest rises and falls in heavy pants. The bed sinks and I don't need to look to see it's Augie beside us. His hand reaches out and strokes her bangs away from her forehead, thankfully the makeup she has on still covers the bruise from earlier.

"Yes, Alpha?"

Fuck, hearing her say that to me is incredible. I can't wait to experiment with our designations, to hear her say *"yes, Alpha"* but not in question, but while she's on her knees between me and Wilder, or tied up at our Prime's mercy while I make her beg to come on my tongue over and over with a toy in her ass and pussy, and her mouth filled with one of her pack's cocks. For now, she'll choke my knot with her pussy while the others watch and wait.

"We need to know if you're on birth control," I say.

She blinks and nods, wetting her lips before she speaks, breaking through the neediness of her Omega. "Yes." Her voice is husky.

"Yes what, sweet girl?" Augie asks.

She turns her head to him, wriggling beneath me as her Omega fights to take over again. "I had the shot, and a check up—" Her words break off with a pained sound that makes all the Alpha's in the room purr loud enough you'd think we put it over the speaker system.

Wilder appears on the other side of me, the mattress sinking beneath his weight. Iris stares up at him and blushes, probably because of the dominance that's leaking off him. It's always like that, but even more now because of the situation we're in and his near rut we only stopped because of the emergency blockers.

"Are you saying you've been tested, Omega?" he asks, placing his hand on her forehead, most likely gauging if she's overheated. She is, and that's because she needs a knot. Her hands now resting on my waist feel like a furnace, and her pussy is hot with need. We can all smell her arousal as much as I feel it every time she pushes her hips up into me.

She bites the inside of her cheek and nods.

"We have been too," he assures her.

Iris exhales a breath and squeezes her eyes shut, most likely due to the pain of a cramp. Wilder has pulled his hand away and I'm able to cup her cheek, forcing her to look at me.

"I'm going to undress you now, Omega. Then the others are going to watch while I fuck you, knot you, and make you feel so good. Any objections?"

"No, Alpha. I want you. Need you."

A low, pleasing growl builds in my chest. I check in with my pack once more to make sure they know not to interfere with me. I don't mind sharing, but I don't want to share her right now. My Alpha needs this to be his time with his Omega.

Mateo's joined us on the bed, sitting next to Augie, his hand kneading the back of his mate's neck in the way he likes to do. There's hunger in both their eyes, but approval and permission as well. Not as if I need it, but I do want it.

I find Wilder's next. We spoke briefly while we waited for Iris to arrive and got the nest ready. Most of the discussion was about the film. We called our assistants and explained the situation, that we'd be delayed at least a week and would deal with the rest later. The time we spent speaking about Iris was us agreeing that she was the most important person in our lives now, and we'd do everything we could to show her how well we can take care of her during her most vulnerable time. After that, we'll continue to show her what kind of Alphas and pack we could be for her. That we want to be her everything like she so clearly already is for us.

My Prime, my director, and more importantly, my best friend, dips his chin with approval. He looks back down at Iris with the kind of devotion he has with everything he cares about in his life, yet somehow deeper.

"Iris," he commands so she looks at him instead of me. "Is there anything you don't want to happen here?"

"Bite," she barely gets out, like it hurts to say it. Probably because her Omega wants to be claimed by her mates. And while there's a twinge of disappointment, I understand why. We need more than our scent match and a sudden heat to make that commitment. Even if I know we all want it.

"You have our word that we won't bite you," Wilder answers.

The rest of us speak out our mutual agreement and with that he shifts back on the bed a bit to give me and Iris more room, the movement my green light to continue with my promise.

Renewed heat builds throughout my body and my canines ache. I remind my Alpha that it's not on the menu, but everything else is. With everything in place now and the words we need spoken out in the air, I peel myself away from Iris to get a good look at her. Her eyes find mine as I drop my hands to the button of her jeans and slowly undo it, followed by the zipper. She pants in anticipation, eyes glazing over as her Omega comes back out to play.

My Alpha perks up, his chant of *"Mine, mine, mine! Claim, claim, claim!"* building in my mind until it's nearly all I hear.

I remove her shoes and strip the fabric that had grown wet with slick from her body, her thick thighs trembling with need and damp with arousal. I groan alongside my packmates when I discover her naked pussy. I have no doubt that her underwear is in either Mateo or Augie's pocket. Not that I can blame them, I would have done the same.

"Beautiful," I say loud enough that she can hear me.

Our Omega's scent fills the air at my praise, and a fresh gush of slick leaks from her plump pussy that's covered in perfectly trimmed dark hair, shiny and soaked by her arousal. I drop her jeans on the ground and wrap my palms around her ankles, tugging her forward so her legs are splayed open and knees are bent over the curved edge of the bed. She squeals at the sudden shift but doesn't struggle or try to cover herself up.

This new angle spreads her pussy lips, more slick producing in preparation for what I promised her I'd do.

"Wilder, help an Alpha out and remove our Omega's shirt while I pet her pretty clit and make her come before she chokes my knot."

"I thought we were watching." Wilder grins.

"If you don't do it, compa, I will," Mateo adds, his voice playful, yet edged with warning that he'll take over if needed.

The threat spurs Wilder into action and he moves so he can look into Iris's eyes. He trails a finger down the column of her neck, right over her scent gland. She gushes more slick, wetting the purple sheets beneath her and turning them a darker color.

I love it. The more we saturate her nest with the scent of her and us, the better. By the end of her heat we'll be glad we paid more money for the mattress with the waterproof cover and the extra sets of linens that sit in the closet on the other side of the room.

Once this heat wave finally passes, maybe she'll be lucid enough for a short tour. I think she'll love the nest we made for her; the colors already suit her. It's like we knew all along she'd end up here, her dark hair and pale skin striking against the plum-painted walls and deep shadows of the room. There are no windows in this suite. The lights are dim, and a canopy draped over the bed is laced with fairy lights that cast a soft golden glow across the sheets and her body. Just enough to see her, not enough to sting our Omega's sensitive eyes while she's in estrous.

Wilder keeps Iris distracted, his fingers teasing the hem of her shirt near her lower belly. I'm grateful for it so I can give my attention back to her needy pussy. I knee her legs apart further with my own, giving me enough space to tease her. I press my thumb against her straining clit, and she bucks upward on the bed. Our packs soothing purrs provide a symphony of comfort, even Augie making a low humming sound that balances out the deeper nature of our Alpha purrs.

Iris whines. "Please, Alpha. Don't tease me."

"I'm not, star. I just need to make sure you're ready to take my knot."

She pouts, bottom lip sticking out. It's fucking adorable, and I want to take that lip into my mouth and bite it.

"I swear I'm ready! Please, Alpha."

I rub slightly faster circles over her sensitive bud. She's not far from coming, and that's all I want her to do before I give her what we both need.

I slide my other hand up her thigh while Wilder removes her shirt, her heavy tits spilling over the cups of the white bra. All our eyes are on the almost naked and squirming Omega, skin flushed pink with desire, belly perfectly soft, decorated in light stretch marks I want to lick.

"Bra too, Wilder."

My order comes out as more of a bark, not that it has an effect on my Prime. He holds back a laugh at my slip up, but follows it, not angry at me for using it. He knows my control is waning, and my Alpha wants what our Omega wants.

I dip my fingers into her pussy. Her inner muscles clench down on my two fingers and I insert a third, moving around in circles timed with my thumb on her clit to stretch her hole wide for me.

She moans and wriggles, on the brink of the release I want from her. Wilder manages to get her out of her bra, breasts freeing from their confines. They're big and round, nipples tight and dark pink, begging to be sucked. Mateo swears under his breath and Augie groans. Wilder eyes me, and the bastard teases his thumb over one of the pert buds. Iris gasps, chest arching for more. I growl at him for touching, but all he does is snicker. That was his way of paying me back for attempting to use a bark on him.

"More, Alpha. Please!" Iris cries, shifting on the bed to try and get more pressure on her clit.

I give her what she wants, pressing my fingers down and thrusting them deeper into her heat. "You going to come for me, my star?"

She moans, nodding her head frantically. Her pussy flutters, trying to suck my hand all the way. It's hot, and the squelching sounds her pussy makes are erotic.

"Do it, Omega. Come for me." My voice is laced with my bark once more but I don't need it. Her chest arches off the bed and her hips thrust forward. Her thighs tremble as her inner muscles clamp down on my fingers, trying to take what they can't provide her.

I remove my slick-soaked fingers, her hooded eyes on mine as I lick them clean, cock jerking as I taste her. It's like the best strawberry I've ever eaten, but even better than that. It's sunshine on my tongue, or the high I get from catching a difficult wave.

I know from this moment on I'm addicted to her. If she wasn't in heat I'd feast on her day and night, allow her to provide me sustenance. Fuck acting, fuck our business, I'll live between her legs and be her servant for the rest of time.

"Alpha." She stretches out for me, eyes hooded and glazed over. I knew it already, but she's fully in heat now. Lost to her hormones and the comfort of being surrounded by pack. The orgasm I just gave her did nothing to take the edge off, and now it's time for her to take my knot.

I shuck off my pants and briefs, my hard cock bobbing free. I fist my searing shaft, hissing at the rough feel of my own hand.

Iris licks her lips and moans as she takes all of me in. My vision blackens at the edges, heat rising from my toes to my head.

"Mine," I grunt.

"Jett," Wilder warns. "Stay in control."

His bark pulls my dark vision back and I inhale. My Alpha wants to rut, to fuck, to breed. But Iris comes first. While it's not uncommon for an Alpha to go into rut during the heat, I don't want to do that now. Not when I'm her first knot, and when I know my pack deserves to be with her too. If I go into a rut, I won't want to share. She'll be mine until it's over, which could last for days.

I shove my Alpha back and maintain control, focusing on Iris. Our eyes stay locked, her silver ones near black with need and desire. She shifts on the bed, fingers gripping the sheets as she opens her thighs wider, pussy dripping obscenely with slick.

"Fuck me, Alpha."

I growl and grip under her knees, pulling her up. I line my cock up with her slit, dragging the tip over her sensitive clit, gathering slick and her cum as I go. I groan at the heat of her, and my balls tighten with need. I drag my head around her clit once more before I line up with her entrance.

Iris moans, her eyes closing. "Eyes on me when I fuck you, Omega."

The moment her lids snap open I sheath my dick inside her in one long stroke, only stopping when my half-inflated knot bumps against her pussy.

"Oh fuck!" she screams, hands gripping the sheets.

"Gods, Omega. You feel—" I can't find the words, because even heaven doesn't describe how she feels. So tight, so hot, so wet.

"Alpha!" she pleads. "I—please—"

I pull out and thrust back into her hard, cutting off her words. She doesn't need to speak or plead anymore. I've got her now.

I wrap her legs around my hips, her greedy hole pulling me in deeper. I grip her inner thighs and plunge, in and out, looking down to where we're joined. My dick gets wetter from her slick after every thrust, her sex already gripping and releasing, waiting for my knot.

I yank her harder down onto my cock, the top part of my knot slipping inside her. Iris wails, hips shifting up to take more of me.

"Ready to come on my knot, Omega?"

"Yes!" she cries.

I wrap her legs around me before I lean forward, keeping my knot just out of her pussy's full grip. Our chests press together, her hard nipples like glass against my pecs. I scent mark her cheek with mine before meeting her eyes. Her hands grip my forearms now bracketing her body, nails digging into my skin so hard I know they will leave a mark. My Alpha is very happy about that, and my cock kicks inside her, knot throbbing.

I circle my hips, pressing forward. She moans, low and guttural, my knot pushing further in, her pussy expanding to take me. I bite the inside of my cheek to keep from coming too soon—I want every drop of cum inside her. I taste the tang of blood and Iris bares down, the last of my knot slipping into her tight heat.

"Fuck," we both groan. I messily find her lips in our first kiss, tongues searching, tasting, and sucking, our bodies connecting in all the ways they possibly can. She opens her mouth to me wider as my knot swells to its full size, pushing and rubbing until we both feel it lock behind her pubic bone, like the sea meeting the sky at the horizon—inevitable.

Iris cries in pure pleasure, body seizing. I pull back and nearly roar as I come. My vision turns white instead of black, fireworks exploding behind my eyes as my balls drain into her. My knot keeping every drop of my spend locked inside her incredible pussy.

Her inner muscles milk me, her thighs shaking around me with her own orgasm. I move one of my hands between us, rubbing her clit, once, twice, before she's coming again. The tight squeeze of her sucking more cum from my body.

I reward her by fucking into her as deep as I can while locked together, moving my hips and dragging out both of our pleasure. My Alpha is more than satisfied with how she screams my name, and how her hands attempt to drag me fully back on top of her as my knot pulses, cock and knot hitting all the right places that make her see stars.

"Jett," she pants.

"You need to come on my knot again, star?"

She nods, hips swiveling.

"Insatiable, Omega." I chuckle.

I press our chests together and pull out as much as I can, knot tugging but unable to slip free. She screams at the sensation and I bite her lower lip, being careful not to break skin and thrust back inside her hard enough her body jiggles beneath me. I do that once—twice—and on the third time she comes again, wailing and muttering curses under her breath.

I know before I finish emptying inside her that her body is finally sated, the heat wave over for now. My cock is spent, and I already feel my knot loosening, but it won't completely go down until her instincts allow her to release me.

I seek out Iris's gaze, only to find her hardly awake, a sleepy, satisfied smile on her freckled face, the scent of strawberry and lemon swirling together in the air.

Gods, how in the world did we get lucky enough to find her? The buzz in my bond says my pack is thinking the exact same thing.

"Jett," Iris says quietly. Heavy eyes barely fluttering open.

"What is it, star?"

"What's your favorite color?"

My brows lift at the randomness of the question, but I answer easily. "Ocean blue."

"Like your eyes." She smiles wider as her eyelids fall closed. "Mine is purple."

My heart quickens at her admission. Not only because we chose different colors of purple for her nest before we found her, but because it suits her and her name.

"Like an iris flower," I hum.

She nods and tries to open her eyes once more to look at me, but I kiss each lid to stop her. "Rest now." I scent mark her cheek and put my lips to the shell of her ear. "I've got you."

And I'm not letting go.

Chapter Thirteen

Mateo

TODAY HAS BEEN AN incredible ride. A stressful one at times, but seeing Iris asleep, wrapped around my friend and packmate, sated and happy, I wouldn't change anything.

Augie runs his hand down my back, leaning his head on my shoulder as the scent of strawberries and lemons lingers around us. It feels good to know my instincts told me she was ours, even before we could scent her and she us, and even better now that she's in the nest we built for her, helping her through her unexpected heat. I'm not even jealous Jett was the first to knot her, all I feel is content. Like a missing piece of my heart has been found and locked into place.

Jett softly tucks a strand of damp hair behind our sleeping Omega's ear. She doesn't stir, being knotted giving her a brief reprieve from the demands of her heat that will only grow the deeper she surrenders to estrous.

"You did good," Wilder quietly praises from his spot on the other side of the bed.

"Did you just compliment Jett on his knotting skills, compa?" I smirk.

"He did," Jett mutters. "But that's nothing new."

Wilder grins back, our Prime looking more like himself again. I'm glad for it, and I know it helps that Iris is here now and safe, no longer on set and in the proximity of other Alpha's.

There's a lull of silence as we all take a moment to watch Iris sleep. Jett has shifted them on their sides, one of her thick thighs draped over his to hold him close. I'd offer to get a blanket and cover up their nudity, but when an Omega is in heat their body temp isn't normal, and as Alpha's we already run hot. Luckily our pack isn't shy about our bodies or having sex in front of each other so there's no need. Especially since I can already smell her pheromones spiking again, and soon she'll be awake and begging for another knot. Hopefully mine.

"Mateo," Wilder says, his tone more serious now.

I meet his hazel gaze. "Yes?"

"Can you and Augie fill us in on what happened after we left? Iris was distressed when she got here."

A bite of annoyance claws in my gut but I shove it down. I love Wilder, and I know his Alpha is more present than usual because of the situation, but my Alpha is too, and he doesn't like the insinuation of his question.

Augie clears his throat, his hand that was on my back reaching for mine on the bed and squeezing it. I lace our fingers together, taking the comfort my mate is offering me. He's always so in tune with me and knows exactly what I need.

"We eased her through her first heat wave," Augie answers for me. "I used my mouth and fingers and Mateo kissed her. I can go further into detail if you'd like, Alpha."

Pride wells in my chest alongside amusement, getting rid of the annoyance. Wilder swallows, the veins in his throat bulging. He takes a long moment, staring at the both of us before he lets out a tight exhale and spears his hand through his already mussed hair.

"I'm sorry, I'm being an asshole."

"You are, but this is a unique situation," I say.

He nods. "Still. I'm sorry, I shouldn't have phrased the question like that. I have no doubt the two of you took care of her. My Alpha is still agitated, and having all the information will help."

I focus on calming myself, keeping Augie's hand in mine while I look back down at our Omega. With all the excitement and pheromones in the air, it was almost easy to forget the strange interaction we had in the car. Almost.

Iris mutters something but doesn't wake, burying her face into Jett's neck and inhaling deeply. He holds her closer, kissing her cheek and keeping her body pressed to his. When she's settled, Jett looks up at us.

"Before anyone says another word," he says in a hushed tone, his southern drawl slipping through. "Right before the heat wave took her under, she told me she's touch-starved."

A purr springs to life from my chest at the same time Wilder's does. My eyes meet Augie's, his green ones passing on his thoughts without me having to ask.

"Did she mention that to you both as well?" Wilder asks.

I shake my head. "No, but she did get upset in the car. She said she had something to tell us—that could have been it."

"When she wakes up, tell her your favorite color too, Wilder," Augie says. "She asked Mateo and I in the car. She'll want to know."

"I was wondering why she asked Jett that question."

"I think it's her way of knowing us better, even if it's something small," my mate adds.

My heart skips a beat at Augie's perceptiveness, and I bring his hand up to my lips and kiss the knuckles, the lingering scent of her slick embedded into his skin along with his basil. It smells like sin, and I can't wait to taste his cum and hers together. I know it will be the best thing I've ever tasted.

Before I can get too carried away and lick his hand or pin him to the bed, I address the other two Alphas.

"I think Augie is right. It's understandable given how quickly everything happened." I know I'm already craving information about the Omega in my packmates arms.

I want to know about her past, why she got into acting, what her favorite food is, and what she likes to drink since she doesn't drink coffee, and if she likes to read like I do. And in turn, I want to tell her everything about me, spend hours with her and

Augie, bring her to meet my dad and moms not far from here in Pasadena, and travel to my extended family's home in Mérida, Mexico. I already know everyone is going to love her like they love Augie and the rest of my pack.

"Okay," Wilder says. "I'll make sure to tell her. Do you think there was something else bothering her?"

"If she said she's touch starved, her hormones are most likely out of whack," Augie adds. "Depending on when her last heat cycle was and how long she's been taking suppressants, it could impact the length of her heat and how severe it is."

My eyebrows shoot up in surprise. "Since when do you know this information, mi amor?"

He smiles sheepishly and he uses his free hand to push his glasses up the bridge of his nose. "I heard her tell Jett and looked it up while…" He looks down at Iris with lust but doesn't finish his sentence.

I hold in a laugh and amusement from the others shoots through our bond. Only my mate would Google while Jett was fucking our Omega into overwhelming pleasure. I may have a strong hold on my Alpha, but I wasn't paying attention to anything except every expression and noise Iris was making while she was being taken care of—I know Wilder wasn't either.

I'm about to ask him what else he found out when strawberry perfume bursts around us, hitting me square in the gut. I groan, gripping Augie's hand to keep from pulling Iris into my arms.

Jett soothes his hand down her back, the scent of slick and cum making it obvious that his knot has released and Iris is revving up into another wave of her heat.

My cock throbs and I can scent my own honey pheromones getting stronger.

"Star," Jett croons. "Do you need to be filled again?"

Instead of answering, she whines. I grit my teeth at the noise and look at Wilder. I know I technically don't need his permission to take care of our Omega, but I do it out of respect for him and his position.

In most cases he would have been the first to knot Iris in her very first heat with us in her new nest, but again, this situation is not a normal one. We're also not a pack that necessarily follows traditional ways of pack life. Wilder may be our leader but he's not an asshole who thinks that just because he's the most dominant means he does everything first. The only thing he'll need to do is bite her first, that way our pack link is as solid as it can be. Then the rest of us can bite her in any order.

I clench my jaw, teeth throbbing. I cannot think about bites right now. Not when we haven't even had a chance to speak to Iris for more than a few words on set and in the car. We also told her we wouldn't bite her, and I'd never break her trust like that.

"You good, Mateo?" Wilder asks, the question carrying more weight than the words themselves.

I swallow and dip my head. "I'm good."

He looks away from me and down at Iris. Jett is gently peeling her fingers from his shoulders. Her nails have left crescent marks and her nose is buried into his scent gland. She keens, hips thrusting forward in search of a knot.

Jett groans when she shifts against his already hard cock. Alphas are made for Omegas, and during a heat we're constantly ready to go. That way the Omega is always satisfied and chances of pregnancy are high. The image of Iris, belly growing round with our child, hits me hard and I stifle a groan.

I can't think about that right now. While it's a wonderful image, it's not happening now or maybe ever. Regardless, the idea of Iris pregnant is one I love picturing, and it makes me even harder than before and my Alpha far too excited.

Contrólate, Alpha. If I don't, I'll fall into a rut. The last thing any of us need today is another close call. Iris, Augie, Jett—even Wilder—they need me present and in control.

"I know, I know. You're going to get what you need," Jett soothes. "Mateo is going to help you. You remember him, don't you Omega?"

Jett lifts her chin up to look at me and I see her spark of recognition before she nuzzles. While Iris will still have some awareness during her heat waves, with her Omega taking charge sometimes it's easy to get confused and lost in the moment. Just like when an Alpha is lost to rut. You're there, but you feel as if you're not and it's hard to think straight. Needless to say, I'm glad Iris and her Omega know who I am at the moment. It will get harder for her as the days go on.

Augie lets go of my hand so I can hold my arms out to her. "Can I take care of you, mi conejita?"

She scrunches her nose, pupils dilating as she observes me. Or should I say her Omega does. There's a half second where I wonder if she's going to say no for some reason, but then she's pushing out of Jett's arms, nearly kneeing him in the balls and almost knocking Augie off the bed.

I'd find it funny, and would have probably laughed, if I didn't have a very naked and very hot-to-the-touch Omega now in my arms, her lips sealing over my scent gland and sucking so hard I see stars.

"Mierda," I groan. "Tómatelo con calma, nena." *Take it easy, baby.*

"No!" she nips at me, clearly understanding me. I'd assumed she could understand Spanish after our earlier interactions, but it makes me happy to know she does. When she's out of her heat, I'll find out how much she knows and if she can speak it like the rest of my pack can—Augie being the most fluent.

I purr louder for her, but the sound does the opposite of calming her. She scrapes her teeth over my throat and my dick twitches in my pants.

"Augie." I find his gaze. He's moved so he's sitting further up the bed now, leaning on the edge of the custom headboard upholstered in deep purple velvet. It was sweet of him to give us room, but I'm a man who likes to take time with his meals. Savor them, find every note of flavor in each bite. And this will be my only first time with our Omega. I'm going to make it so Iris remembers every bit of it, even through her heat haze.

"Yeah, baby?" he asks. His tone is breathless, lustful. My delicious mate came in his pants earlier while eating Iris out. It was hot to watch, but just like the rest of the pack, our Omega's heat calls to him even as a Beta. He's no longer satisfied, his cock straining against the pair of jeans he found on set.

"I want you to keep her happy while I get her ready for my knot."

The command to my mate sobers Iris and she pulls back, pouting adorably. "I'm ready now."

I chuckle and kiss her nose before trailing down over her cheekbone until I reach her mouth. I kissed her on set but it was at an awkward angle. And what can I say, I may be a patient Alpha but I'm not an idiot. I'm going to make out with my Omega any chance I get.

I seal my lips over hers and she isn't shy, opening up to me without a fight. Our tongues slide together, the strawberry taste of her sweet and tangy, along with a hint of Jett's lemon. It's delicious, so good I could kiss her for hours on end. But she needs more from me than just a heated open-mouthed kiss.

I pull back and nibble at her lower lip. "I'm going to lay you down, mi conejita."

With a plea, she once again tries to pull me back, but I'm stronger than her and lower her until she's lying flat on the bed, breasts flushed and chest heaving.

"Shh, I promise you're going to get what you need. Have patience," I murmur. I do know what she needs and I have an idea—and it involves more than just me. Soon she'll be so full and occupied she won't even remember having to pout and beg.

I glance at Augie, my eyes taking in his short breaths and aching dick that he's palming through his jeans before I gesture to Iris's mouth. He slowly smiles, using his free hand to push his glasses up the bridge of his nose before nodding.

I look at my other packmates. The bed is plenty big enough for all of us. In the time I've had Iris in my arms, Jett has propped himself against the center of the headboard, not bothering to put any clothes on, his cock and knot swollen again. Wilder is still in the spot he was before, focused on Iris as if he's trying to read her mind. It's interesting to see him now, no longer on the verge of rut. Instead he's in leader mode like he is on set. Though his muscles are still tense.

I tap into my pack bond with him and feel his anxiety but also his relief at Iris here safe in the nest with us. I know he's holding back from barking at me to give her what she needs now, but even though we personally have never been intimate together, he understands how I operate and the non-Alpha part of him knows I'll deliver. I'm grateful he's no longer trying to take over or barking like he was when we arrived. But I can throw him a bone.

"Omega," I say as I shift her up on the bed until she's closer to where Augie was. He's standing near the side of the bed now, removing his clothes to reveal his lean, toned body and the long, hard cock I love so much.

"Augie is going to fuck your mouth, and Wilder is going to suck your tits while Jett gets his cum ready for you. How does that sound?"

She moans loudly and bobs her head along with a yes that spills from her lips. Slick floods from her ready pussy and her strawberry perfume fills the air in an almost jammy scent that makes my mouth water and the rest of my pack's pheromones go wild.

My own honey scent is thick and syrupy, mixing with Jett's tart lemon, Wilder's fresh mint, and Augie's earthy basil. It smells exquisite. Like pack.

"Please," Iris squirms. "I need it all. Need you—need your knot, Alpha. It hurts."

A low growl builds in both Wilder and Jett's chests and my own Alpha gets pissed at me, my cock protesting painfully as if to say, *"stop this already and fuck our Omega."*

"Augie," I bark. He's moving before I can say more. He remains standing off to the side of the bed but puts one knee above Iris's head so his straining shaft is aligned with her mouth. He takes his hand and guides her face to look at him. He strokes her cheek lovingly, with the kind of reverence only he can have.

"Open your mouth, Omega," I demand before my mate can.

Iris doesn't need to be told twice. She opens wide and Augie guides his weeping head into her offered hole. I don't know where to look, but my gaze flits to Augie's face at the moment her tongue connects with his cock. His eyes roll into the back of his head and Iris moans, more of her perfume thickening in the air.

"Fuck, sweet girl. That feels so good," he groans.

The sound of her sucking reaches my ears and I shift away enough I can finally remove the clothes that have become insufferable against my skin. Iris, now occupied with our Beta's cock, thankfully doesn't miss my brief absence. Wilder takes the opening to move closer to Iris. His focus is now on the job I've given him and satisfying our Omega through her burning heat wave.

I shuck off my shirt and pants, my erection tenting my boxers. I briefly spy Jett; he's stroking his thick shaft, eyes on Iris as if she's hung the moon. His star. It's a sweet nickname, and I'm sure it has to do with the fact she's now the star of his show—our show. In more ways than one.

Wilder's loud and rumbling purr spurs to life like his old motorcycle he's got stashed in the garage somewhere. Iris produces more slick, rubbing her wet thighs together, her sucking becoming louder as Wilder reaches out to palm her large breasts.

I've never been attracted to my Alpha packmates more than platonically, but even I can't deny seeing her heaving tits gripped beneath Wilder's massive, tattooed hands is sexy.

Iris arches her chest into his touch, and Augie reaches out to hold her head on his cock to support her so she doesn't accidentally hurt herself or him.

"Goddamn, little Omega," Wilder growls. "I can't wait to fuck your tits." He pinches one of her nipples and she cries out around Augie's arousal. "I bet these would look pretty pierced too." He flicks the hard bud he just pinched and she gushes more slick.

"I think she liked that idea," I comment as I remove my briefs, jacking my heated shaft in my palm. Pre-cum leaks from the head, and if I had more time I'd let her take turns sucking both me and Augie off. But that will have to come later. Our pack's cum is good for her during a heat, and can help sate cramps, but it doesn't do what a knot can. What coming inside her can.

Wilder alternates to the other nipple, pinching it hard so she pulls back on Augie's hands, popping off his cock to gasp. The action creates a trail of saliva that drips from the ruddy head of his dick and on to the edge of the bed.

"Do you like the idea of me piercing these, Omega?" Wilder leans down and sucks one of her sensitive nipples.

"Yes!"

He hums and pulls back, pinching both between his fingers now and rolling them. "They'd look so good on these big tits. Make you more sensitive too."

I chuckle. Wilder would know since the man is packing hardware under his clothes, something Iris will eventually find out.

"Gods," Iris writhes. "More!"

Wilder takes her nipple back into his mouth, sucking hard enough that nearly all the darkened skin of her areola disappears between his lips.

My cock pulses in my hand, knot already enlarged and heavy. I pump my shaft several times and squeeze my knot, feeling my orgasm a breath away. I pull away the contact before I can come, sweat dripping down my back. My balls pinch at the loss of release, but I revel in the pain of it. In the denial of my orgasm. It's going to make the moment I knot Iris that much more intense.

"Omega." I lace her designation with a heavy bark, enough that the air around us pulls tight. Her moan cuts off, her hands gripping the sheets beneath her so tight her knuckles are white.

"Did I say you could stop sucking our Beta's cock?"

"No, Sir."

Mierda. Every male in the room groans, our scents spiking. We all liked that. A submissive omega is like waving a steak in front of a dying person. Even Augie liked it, but probably because he loves calling me Sir when we're playing with our power dynamics.

Augie turns her head back to his cock and Iris takes it between her lips like she was born to do it. I wet my lips and check in with Jett. He's still stroking his cock languidly while watching the scene before him, the tattoos normally covered by wardrobe or makeup littering his arms and chest.

I move up onto the bed, the mattress dipping beneath my weight. Iris feels it and drops her legs open obediently, an Omega spreading for her Alpha. I swear under my breath at the beautiful sight. Her weeping pink slit wet and ready, slick covering her thighs along with Jett's seed dripping from deep within. My knot spasms with need. Need to come. Need to fill her, breed her.

I bend forward and inhale long and deep, taking in her sweet yet earthy smell. I ignore the sucking of Wilder's lips around her nipples, the dirty sounds of her taking my mate's cock in her mouth, and Jett's breathing. I focus on her wet pussy, how this amazing female we just met is so willing to trust us. Opening her body like a flower to me so I can smell, touch, taste, and fuck.

I grip her full thighs in my palms and spread her wider, groaning as my cock drags against the sheets. Iris whines, her body beginning to tremble. I know she needs a knot, and I want to give it to her. I had plans to do more of what Augie and Jett have already done. Stretch her with my fingers, make her come before I shove my knot inside her. But all my well-practiced restraint is quickly crumbling.

My Alpha pushes beneath the surface with more strength than he ever has before and I growl, shoving him back down.

"Mateo..." Augie's strained voice meets my ears but it's hard to hear. "Mateo, are you—"

I ignore him. No, I will not go into rut. But I'm not going to deny myself any longer. I bend down and with a flat tongue I lick from the bottom of her pussy and up to her clit, tasting the combined essence of her and Jett. My cock jerks and I do it again, Iris's hips thrusting up into my mouth. I pull back and swat her clit lightly so she cries out, pulling off Augie's cock once more.

"Mateo," Wilder warns.

I glare at him. Not even needing to say to him that I know his brand of dominance is similar to mine. He'd have smacked Iris's clit harder than I would have. I have no doubt that before this heat is over he'll have her presenting in the middle of the bed, ass in the air, red from his spanks. I may not have seen him do it, but I know what he likes—heard the stories of his escapades with Jett. So he can fuck right off.

I lick her clit again, then pull back. Iris whines and I nip at her ripe inner thigh before connecting with her blown out pupils, no silvery-grey left in sight.

"Get on your hands and knees, Omega."

Chapter Fourteen

Iris

Hands help me flip. There's an innate part of me that wants to present, to press my cheek into the soft sheets and show my dripping pussy, but the teasing Alpha didn't tell me that's what he wanted.

"Hands and knees," a voice reminds me.

Yes, that was the command. My breasts sway as I get into position, my nipples wet from the big-tattooed Alpha's mouth. The cool air makes them even more sensitive and I wish his strong hands would touch and pinch them again. Tease me like he was while the Beta's cock was in my mouth. I lick my lips, wanting to taste him again. To feel his heated shaft slide in and out while he holds my face firm.

My eyes drift up to the Alpha who took care of me before. The one who smells and tastes like lemons. *Jett*. Yes, that's who it is. He's stroking his cock that's curved at the tip, dark blond hair no longer perfect. I whimper at the sight of him and he smiles in a sweet lopsided way that has my heart thumping wildly in my chest. I shift forward so I can crawl to him and sit on his growing knot, but strong hands on my thighs pull me back.

I expel a sound of discontent but don't have time to complain because the Beta turns my head toward him and presses his thumb to my swollen lips. "Hey there, sweet girl, you ready to be knotted by Mateo?"

Mateo. He's the sexy dark-haired Alpha who smells of honey and calls me a bunny. My nose scrunches and the Beta smiles warmly, his glasses slightly askew on his face and hair a mess. I'd reach up and fix them if I didn't need his cock so much. I nod in a response and open my lips with the gentle pressure of his finger.

"Such a good girl for your pack."

I preen at the praise, loving that I have a pack.

You don't, the rational part of me, the Iris that is hovering beneath the surface, retorts.

I whine and the Beta mistakes it for need. He slides the head of his dick between my lips, his herby flavor exploding over my tongue. I hollow my cheeks, falling into the feel of him using me. His warm hands cup my face, this new position allowing me to take more of him into my mouth. I love how the vein running along the underside of it feels against my tongue, and it makes me greedy for more.

Strong hands run down my back, the rough pads of their fingertips making me arch into them. The bed shifts but I can't see what's happening since my mouth and head are being held in place. The touch on my back drifts to my ass and my cheeks are spread. There's the sensation of something cool on my back entrance, and I think the Alpha Mateo and the big one who was playing with my tits are talking.

Wilder, my brain reminds me. *And the Beta is Augie*. He's the sweetest—and he tastes yummy too.

"Mateo is going to put a plug in your ass," Augie says, slowly inching deeper into my mouth. The head of his cock hits the back of my throat, but not hard enough for me to gag. "That okay?"

Anything would be okay right now. But I nod and he guides my head back then forward again, fucking my face with gentle precision. I want him to do it faster, harder, use me until he comes and I can swallow it down. But I let him have the lead and enjoy being taken care of for once.

Mateo's fingers prod at my back hole and another wave of slick drips down my thighs. His fingers disappear for a moment then swipe through the slick before returning to my tight ring of muscle. I keen, the strong hands that can only belong to the Alpha Wilder reaching under me to play with my tits again. He growls low and sexy beside me and presses a kiss to my shoulder.

"You're doing so well, little Omega." I shiver at the Prime's praise, his dominance leaking from every word. I arch my ass even higher and suck harder on the Beta's cock.

Augie groans. "I'm not gonna last much longer, Mateo."

"Don't you dare come yet, mi amor."

He whimpers, the sound making my clit pulse. He slows the movements of my head on his cock and my nipples are pinched hard at the same time the cool tip of the plug breaches my asshole. Fingers touch my clit, giving it just the right amount of pressure, and like a tidal wave, an orgasm hits me.

I scream around the sweet Beta's cock and he pulls me back just enough the crown lays on the tip of my tongue so I can breathe. There's rumbles of purrs and pleased words, and while the orgasm feels nice and there's now the weight of a plug in my ass, I need a knot. My pussy flutters around nothing and my lower stomach cramps.

I'm about to beg, but I don't need to. A cock is lined up at my entrance, one hand gripping my hip so hard I know it will bruise. *Good.*

Augie pulls his shaft from my mouth and I'm shoved forward from the strength of the cock—Mateo's cock—now sheathed inside me, the swollen knot just stretching my opening but not going all the way in and his honey scent enveloping me.

"Fuck!" I scream. "Oh, fuck!"

The mix of the teasing Alpha's sheer length, the burning stretch of his knot trying to work itself inside me, and the plug in my ass is nearly too much. When his knot is fully in, it's going to push me to my limit.

"Just wait until it's two cocks inside you, little Omega," Wilder growls against my ear, and I realize I said that out loud.

"We're gonna knot your cunt and tight ass so good you won't be able to see straight."

"Yes," I find myself moaning. "Please."

There's a swat on my ass and my back dips. "You ready for all of me, mi conejita?"

Mateo grips my hips with his hands, pulling me back so more of his knot slips in. All I can do is nod and push back, trying to take more of him. He's so thick it burns, but I need it. Need his knot, his cum.

"Play with her clit, Wilder," he says to the Prime. His attempt at dominance over the stronger Alpha is attractive in ways I can't explain, especially when Wilder does what he asks, and I cry out.

Mateo circles his hips, speaking to me in Spanish. I like it. His words are soothing, full of praise and calm. The moment my muscles relax, he pulls his cock nearly all the way out before he slams back in in one long thrust. His hips slap against the backs of my thighs and ass, his balls smacking my pussy.

"Oh, Omega!" Mateo groans and I howl in pure pleasure when his knot pops behind my pubic bone and locks into place. It swells rapidly, gearing for its release. The heat and pressure of it hits all the right spots inside my pussy that make me scream.

"That's it! Take my Alpha knot, milk it dry," he barks. I come, inner muscles fluttering and squeezing around him, triggering his orgasm. His hot seed shoots deep inside my needy pussy, filling me up. The feel of it is searing yet wonderful, and my toes curl against the mattress.

Before I know it, I'm begging for more, not knowing what I'm asking for. I'm so full, so hot, the cramps in my stomach abating as I orgasm around him, the muscles of my ass gripping the plug like it's also a knot, but there's something missing.

I whine and Mateo swivels his hips to continue our pleasure now that we're locked together.

"Give it to her, mi amor. Feed her your cum."

The Beta takes my chin and I open my mouth without him asking. His cock presses in, thrusting with a strength he didn't use before. I love it, want him to face fuck me hard and make me take it. It's been so long since I've been manhandled and used, and I want it all. I want to taste his release and see the pleasure that I gave him on his features.

"Suck, sweet girl. Make me give it to you."

I do as he asks, the Prime's fingers on my clit moving in perfect circles with just the right amount of pressure. I faintly hear the sound of skin on skin and quickening breaths, and I don't have to see to know it's coming from Jett stroking his dick. I wish I could see it, but I want to taste Augie's cum.

I suction my lips harder on his cock and he groans, cupping the back of my head and sliding me down until my nose is by his pubic bone. He thrusts, hitting the back of my throat, shaft tightening and twitching.

"I'm coming, Omega."

He grunts and the taste of freshly muddled basil overwhelms my mouth, too much to swallow. It leaks from the corners of my lips but I don't pull away, wanting every drop I can get in my stomach.

I breathe through my nose and swallow until there's nothing left. Augie praises me while sliding me off his softening shaft. I look up at him as he cleans the cum that slipped out of my mouth with his thumb, then he feeds it to me with hooded eyes.

I suck the pad into my mouth, his skin adding a hint of salt. My moan of delight gets cut off when my clit is pinched and Mateo thrusts deep, grunting husky words of pleasure as his knot lodges so far inside me I see stars. I orgasm again, every part of my body trembling.

Another hand, one that smells of lemons grips my chin. I look up into Jett's blue eyes. He's kneeling in front of me now with his cock ready for me. The fat tip ruddy and leaking.

"Open, star. I've got more for you," his slightly-twanged voice demands.

I stick my tongue out flat, and he pumps his cock until his hot cum splashes over my tastebuds. The lemon of him mixes with the basil flavor still on my tongue and I can't help but think how good it tastes together. I manage to bring one hand up and wrap it around his cock over his hand. He grunts in surprise then moans deeply as I squeeze my hand over his to get more of his cum.

"Hungry, Omega," the Prime chuckles. "Give it all to her, Jett."

Jett says something to him but I'm too focused on his cock and getting every last drop. I seal my lips over the slit and suck. He cups the back of my head and grips my hair, the sting on my scalp making me shiver.

"So good, Omega. So fucking good."

I hum around Jett and take everything I can. When there's no more left and my orgasm has faded into small aftershocks, the wave of tiredness that hits me is fast and quick. My eyelids droop and the muscles in my arms become boneless.

Before long I'm being gently moved, Mateo's knot still lodged inside my body and the plug in my ass. It feels good, comforting in a way. But not as good as his arms locked around my stomach and the kiss he lays on my neck as I fall into a deep and dreamless sleep, the scent of pack surrounding me.

I wake up no longer knotted and to the quiet sounds of snoring and slow breaths. I blink my eyes open and closed several times before staring up at the canopy above covered in twinkling fairy lights. I didn't have much time to look at the nest before my heat waves took over, but I smile when I take in the tiny yellow lights.

My solo nest in my condo in Burbank has similar fairy lights, but the nest as a whole is not nearly as nice. It was good enough for me and pleased my Omega, resting on a queen-sized mattress with lots of blankets, but this…

This one's better.

Of course this one's better, I answer my Omega mentally. It's not only bigger, but it smells like pack. Lemons, honey, basil, strawberry and the faint scent of mint. Like the garnish on top of a drink. I want more of that scent.

The big-tattooed Alpha. Need him.

I squeeze my thighs together at the thoughts of Wilder now swimming in my mind and exhale softly. I look to the side but don't see him. He was next to me before; I could feel him touching my cheek as I fell asleep on Mateo's knot, but he's not there. I frown, running my hand over the spot on the bed that's cool to the touch. He's the only one left of the Alphas to knot me. I've only tasted his kiss, and I need more.

That's what I said.

I roll my eyes at my hussy of an Omega, who's also very sassy in heat. Well to me at least, she's very sweet and submissive to the pack. But it's nice that she's giving me a slight reprieve from her shenanigans. I know it won't be for long before she's taken over again. With the thoughts of Wilder, there's a simmering heat burning in my belly, but that could also be because I have to go to the bathroom.

I blink back up at the twinkling lights, sending a silent plea to my Omega to behave for a bit longer while I go clean up, and that the rest of the pack I smell around me remains sleeping. I don't need to see myself to know I'm sticky and sweaty. My Omega likes it, wants to be messy and caked with cum and slick. But my rational brain, the Iris/professional actor part of me, doesn't.

With some clarity, the thoughts I had in the car on the way here creep back into my mind like a dark and ominous shadow. Pack Quinn are our scent matches. We found them. But I've also ruined their movie. I highly doubt they're going to want me when this is all over and pheromones have cleared.

I shut my eyes and ignore the protests of my Omega. She believes the Alphas and the Beta think very differently. And maybe they do, but our designations will always default to their instincts, whereas the people: Wilder, Jett, Mateo, and August, could very well not agree.

After another minute I open my eyes again and slowly sit up, glad I'm not connected to Mateo at the moment. My body aches in places I forgot existed and the weight of the plug in my ass reminds me of when they put it in. My cheeks burn as the memories of everything my Omega did in this bed flutter through my brain like a leaf in the breeze.

Before I can think too much about it, gravity draws slick and cum from my body, and I cringe. Yes, I definitely need the bathroom. Also, thank fuck for birth control, because there's no way I wouldn't be pregnant with the amount of cum Jett and Mateo already pumped into me.

My omega pouts and I almost laugh. I remind her that we aren't getting pregnant until we're packed up and ready for that responsibility—okay, until I'm ready. I know that my Omega's been ready, but my career has been what's important and I don't regret that in the slightest.

I glance around the lowly lit nest. Jett is lying at the top of the mattress, naked and asleep. I avoid looking at his package because I'm trying to get out of this bed, not trigger another wave. I look beside me where Mateo is sleeping, Augie on the other side of him. The two of them are also naked. Mateo is face up, a corded forearm draped over his eyes and the Beta is koala-beared to his side, glasses nowhere to be found. It's adorable to say the least.

I look back to where Wilder was, a reminder he left at some point. And long enough ago that the bed is cold. My heart sinks and my Omega pouts, but I try not to think too much into it, or the fact he hasn't been inside me yet and his scent is too light in the nest.

He's probably off doing damage control for the havoc I've created. There's also the little fact I lied and said I was on suppressants. Gods, I need to come clean. But I obviously can't do that now.

I slide off the bed, making as little noise as possible, shoving away the pull to immediately dive back in the nest and jump on the nearest cock. I stand naked in front of the mattress and look around the room decorated in various shades of purple. The suite is large and there are no windows, perfect for my sensitive eyes during a heat. The fairy lights and a few shaded lamps in the corners provide the only light, making this place feel like a cozy cave. I look ahead to see large french-style doors that I remember being brought through when I first arrived.

The bathroom won't be out that way so I look to the left and see a small kitchen area with a stainless-steel fridge and a breakfast nook with five chairs. The thoughtfulness they put into the room is amazing, and I feel bad that I'm soiling it. When this is all over, if they ever bring another Omega here, it will have to be completely redone and stripped of my scent. Something that won't be easy to do with all the pheromones I've pumped in this room.

The bridge of my nose stings and I remember I'm not supposed to be thinking about that. Deciding it has to be to the right, I step away from the bed and the sleeping pack. There's a wall that leads to a small hallway and when I reach it I see a door cracked open at the end with light leaking through. My feet carry me faster, and a tugging sensation builds the closer I get to the door. It's odd, but I don't have time to question it because I hear a low and deep voice humming a tune I recognize. An old lullaby I think? One my mom used to sing to me when I was a child.

I should turn around and find another bathroom to use, but instead I step closer, the drum of water hitting tile from a shower becoming evident. I push the door slightly wider so I can see in, stepping just enough into the bathroom. The tile under my feet is warm, and satisfaction works its way into my being. The floors of the nest must be heated.

They're perfect, my Omega preens.

And rich. Heated floors in Los Angeles are not easy to come by. But my toes are not complaining.

The humming is replaced by raspy singing, the tone vibrating through me from the souls of my feet all the way to the top of my head.

"Hush now, love, the day is done, sleep will come with the setting sun."

Okay, wow. Wilder is not only an amazing director and business person, but he can sing? It's not perfect by any means, but it's deep and beautiful. Almost haunting.

Slick wets my inner thighs, and I grip the handle of the door in my hand so I don't run into the bathroom.

I swallow hard, eyes finding his body as he continues to sing. He's standing under the spray of a luxurious rainforest shower. The frosted stall is huge, and the light above him is bright enough I can make out his massive, tattooed body. His back is to me, round ass flexing as he scrubs himself down.

Holy shit, are those dimples on his butt?

The scent of strawberries floats around me, and I'm grateful he's under a spray of water and lathering himself up with soap, or there's no doubt in my mind that he'd smell me.

"Dreams will hold you, warm and near, until the morning light appears."

My heart squeezes in my chest, memories of hearing this song as I fell asleep as a child pushing into the forefront of my mind. My mom used to tell me to dream of my future pack, and while I did, more than I ever cared to admit, I also dreamed of my future. Of being a star.

My eyes burn and I take in a sharp breath before I can think about how loud it is. Wilder's body stills and he turns. I close my eyes like a child who believes they can't be seen if they can't see you.

"Iris?"

I know I can't just stand here gripping the door handle with my eyes closed, so I do what an adult would do and open them. My gaze meets Wilder's through the frosted glass. I grit my teeth to keep from closing my eyes again, or gods forbid looking down to his crotch. I already saw his well-sculpted backside and those cute dimples I want to lick; I'll be running straight into the shower if I see his cock right now.

So? my Omega sasses.

She's lost her damn mind now that she has the reins. A little taste of power and a scent-matched pack and everything I've worked for is gone out the window.

"Sorry," I clip out. "I was—"

Wait. What was I doing again?

Wilder doesn't move, doesn't try to cover himself. His eyes remain on mine, and I swear I see the corner of his mouth tipping up into a grin. He's standing far enough out of the spray that the water hits his back but drops cascade down from his hair and beard that both appear darker wet. Seriously, the Alpha looks like he just stepped out of every wet dream I had as a teen. One where the tatted bad boy sweeps me off my feet and takes me for a ride on the back of his bike.

Okay, let's be honest. I've had that fantasy as an adult too.

I swallow, frozen to my spot. I tell my feet to move, to speak, to do anything, but every time I try to turn to leave it's like an invisible force is making me stay put.

"Do you need to use the bathroom?" He runs a hand over his hair, then down his face, clearing any rouge water.

Oh right. That's what I came here to do.

I nod dumbly and he points behind me. "Just head toward the sink and go right. You'll see the toilet. It has a door you can close for privacy."

My skin burns and I nod again. "T-thanks."

He steps back under the spray and a flare of rejection stings in my gut. That's idiotic considering I walked in here on him in the shower. He's also being considerate. What did I expect him to do, bark at me and tell me to join him?

My clit pulses at the idea but before I flood the space with my perfume while I stand here awkwardly and stare, naked and covered in slick and cum I might add, and a plug still in my ass, I scurry toward the bathroom.

Safely inside, I shut the door behind me and begin to cry.

Chapter Fifteen

Wilder

I REST MY FOREHEAD on the cool tile of the shower wall, clenching my fists at my side. I'm fighting to keep my Alpha down. It was hard enough to walk away from her while she slept, but now that she's in the bathroom with me, and we're alone, my Alpha wants to chase after her and claim her. Put my mark on her neck so she can never leave.

I run my tongue over my canines and take a few calming breaths. I've taken enough rut blockers today to put down a pack of wolves, and I can't take anymore. It's why I left the nest when I did. I have a lot of control, but having our scent-matched Omega in the nest we built in hopes of finding her one day, smelling like pack and the best strawberry dessert I could imagine, I had to get out so I didn't lose myself and claim her. It's the one request she had of us, and I'm not going to let her or my pack down.

I step under the spray and turn the water near-scalding. The burning water is painful, but it's what I need. A reminder that my body is my vessel and I'm the one in control of it. I don't have to fall into my baser urges. Iris is here, she willingly came to our home, to our nest. *Her* nest. She's not going to suddenly disappear—at least not yet. Not until her heat is over and we have to have some real conversations about the future. Hopefully she'll stay and ask us to be her pack.

She is pack.

I grit my jaw, ignoring my Alpha. I know she *is* pack. But that's not what I'm worried about. It's been only twenty-four hours since we've met. I haven't even been able to tell her my favorite color yet. But hopefully I can rectify it soon along with everything I've done wrong, including acting like an Alpha-hole. Not to mention, I think I'm the one who threw her into heat. My near rut and the way I manhandled her most likely set her off, or helped the process.

There's also the fact she mentioned she's touch starved. Even though she couldn't scent us, nor could we at the beginning, our Alpha's and Beta recognized her and her Omega recognized us. She needed to be taken care of, and her Omega took over and did it in the best way she knew how.

I turn off the water, my skin red from the heat of the water. I grab a towel and dry off before wrapping it around my waist. Iris didn't leave the wash closet yet, and while part of me wants to leave her in peace, my Alpha stops me.

She needs you.

Anxiety builds in my chest, and I step closer to the door she's behind. She's been in there for a while and in my mind all I can picture is her in another wave of heat, suffering on the floor, begging for me.

"Iris?" I call out.

There's no answer, which does nothing but put the fear of the gods in me. I place my hand on the handle and use my other to knock.

"Iris?" I yell louder. "Are you alright?"

I press my ear to the door after another second and that's when I hear it, a sniffle and the low keen of an Omega whine.

"Omega, can you open the door?" I don't lace it with a bark, even if my Alpha wants to. I don't know what's upsetting her and I don't want to make it worse. There's a pause after my question, followed by what sounds like a hiccup.

"Iris," I coax. "I'm going to open the door so I can help you."

I wait a few seconds for her to protest, but when the only answer is another hiccup followed by a sob, my heart breaks and I turn the handle. The sight that greets me is one I both expected to find but hate that I did.

Iris is seated on the floor in front of the toilet, legs hugged to her chest as she cries. I slowly walk in, trying to be as non-threatening as possible. Which is hard to do when you look like me, but I manage it by holding my Alpha back and relaxing my muscles.

"Little Omega," I say quietly. "What's wrong?"

My question only makes her cry harder, and I'll admit I'm out of my element here. I fix problems every day on set and in our business, but Mateo and Augie—even Jett—are much better at handling emotions. But I'm here now, and my Alpha wants me to help our Omega.

I want to help her.

My nostrils flare to scent her, see if she's in a heat wave again. But while it smells of her in here, it's not sweet and syrupy like before, instead it's sour. Her distress has changed her scent.

"I'm fine," she whimpers. "You can go."

"I can't do that, Iris. I need to know what's wrong."

She pries her face from her knees and glares at me with her watery eyes and tear-stained cheeks. The anger in it surprises me.

"You don't want me, so you can go."

I cock my head, brow knitting in confusion. "That's not true."

Fat tears trail down her cheeks and I cautiously take a step forward. Her lip quivers and her nose scrunches. Several emotions I can't read without a bond in place flash through her grey eyes before she blinks, swallowing hard. When she opens her eyes they're clearer, and a pink flush rises in her cheeks.

"I'm sorry. I don't know why I said that."

"Because it's how you feel."

She shakes her head. "My Omega, she's—she's unhinged."

I smile despite the situation. "I can relate to that. My Alpha is the same."

Iris wipes at her cheeks and smiles back at me, the sight healing a bit of my cracked heart. There isn't space for me to join her on the floor so I squat instead, the towel around my waist hardly covering me. "Can you tell me why your Omega feels that way?"

Iris fights to keep her eyes on my face and I'd smile wider if this wasn't a serious conversation.

"It's ridiculous. I swear, it's just all the hormones."

I slowly reach out, and when Iris doesn't stop me I gently place my hand on her shoulder, the contact immediately calming my Alpha. Her muscles relax too and her sour scent begins to sweeten again.

"Nothing you will say to me will be ridiculous. I would love to know so I can make it better."

"Promise you won't laugh?"

"I would never," I say honestly.

She nibbles her lower lip before she finally responds. "I think since you were gone from the nest when I woke up, then you were in the shower and you didn't invite me in, it felt like you didn't want me. Then I came in here and my Omega decided that maybe you were trying to wash our scent away and I lost it."

Fuck. I really screwed up, but I'm going to do what I said and make it better.

"Omega." The tone of my voice is firm. "Don't for a second think I don't want you. That I don't want your scent covering every inch of me."

"Then why?" she asks before she can stop herself.

"Because." I wipe away the remaining tears from her cheeks. "I showered so I could get myself together."

"You seem together to me. You haven't even knotted me."

Her honesty, the mention of knotting—my cock goes painfully hard, and my desire to take her is stronger, if that's even possible.

"My pack needed you."

"And you don't?"

Our eyes remain connected, and it's taking everything in me not to pin her to the ground and fuck her in front of the goddamn toilet to show her how wrong that statement is. But she deserves better than that.

I cup her cheek. "I need you more than I need air, Iris Walker."

"Then show me. Show my Omega."

I don't hesitate in my next movements. I stand and pull her up with me, yanking her so her naked body is flush with mine, only the towel separating my hard cock from her warm heat. She lets out a yelp and perfume explodes around us like an invisible bomb, removing all traces of the sourness that was there before.

A groan builds in my throat and I lean down, pulling her up by the biceps at the same time so she can meet my lips. She opens for me readily, my tongue dominating hers in a rough kiss.

Our first kiss was heated and quick; this one is slow and passionate, yet no less dominant. I control the movement, the timing, and I don't let her up for air. Stealing every taste and breath she'll give me as I enjoy the different notes of her. Sweet, earthy, and all mine.

Iris whimpers against my lips, grinding her hips over the bulge under my towel. Needing her closer, I glide my hands down her soft skin that's heating under my touch and grip her ass. I hoist her up and she throws her arms around my neck, wrapping her legs around my waist and holding me tight.

We both moan at the closer contact, and slick drenches my towel, seeping through to my throbbing cock. I back up and into the larger part of the bathroom, our tongues continuing to dance together as Iris grinds on me, her heavy tits flatting against my chest that rumbles with a loud purr I can't control.

Fuck, she tastes good. Feels good. But not only is her body getting hotter, her scent is so strong now I know her heat is building up again and she needs more.

"Iris," I pull away. She tries to take my lips back in hers but I don't let her. "Omega, wait."

She whines and it physically hurts me. I press her ass back against the shower door so she's propped up, the glass rattling.

"I'm not rejecting you, but I need to tell you something."

Her eyes meet mine, silver-grey gone again.

"Chocolate brown," I say.

She cocks her head in confusion but doesn't speak.

I reach up and play with a lock of her dark hair. "That's my favorite color."

Her eyes light up before she leans forward. I think she's going to kiss me but she rests her head in the crook of my neck and hugs me. Her legs squeeze impossibly hard around my waist, fingernails gripping into the tops of my shoulders where her hands now rest. I squeeze her back, a bit of my heart both breaking and healing.

I hate that she's touch starved, but my Alpha is preening that he's providing her comfort. That she's happy with me and needs me in this way and her anger is gone. I kiss her neck and hold her tightly. The moment seems to last for hours, yet only a minute passes before she squirms in my arms. She takes in a long breath, then licks up my neck right over my scent gland.

My pheromones go wild, the smell of mint twirling with her strawberry sweetness. She licks me again and tries to hike herself up my body like she's climbing a tree. With all the movement my towel was hanging on by a thread, and that does it in. It falls to the ground, her hot slit connecting with my shaft.

I grunt at the contact, the edges of my vision turning black. Oh fuck.

Mine. My Omega.

Iris gasps and wiggles, seeking me out. "Alpha," she pleads against my neck. "Alpha, please."

She sucks on my scent gland, and I know the moment my Alpha finally gets more control over me, the last of my strength holding me back from a rut falling away like the towel had moments ago.

My fingers grip her round ass cheeks, hard enough I know they'll leave marks. But my Omega doesn't seem to care. She sucks deeply on my scent gland, enough that I know she'll leave a bruise.

My cock kicks up and there's a voice in the back of my head screaming at me to let her go—to get her to my pack so I don't lose it—but I can't. It's too late.

The Omega pulls back like she knows, her own eyes black with lust and the high of her estrous.

"Alpha." Her voice is strangely calm. "I trust you."

I purr loudly, a slow smile pulling at my lips. She knew I needed to hear that. Further proving what my Alpha's been saying all along. This beautiful and talented Omega is meant to be part of Pack Quinn, and even without a bite, I'm going to show her that she belongs to me—to us. She'll never question if I want her again.

I slowly lower her down my body until her feet are planted on the ground. Her brow furrows for a moment but I don't give her time to think. I brush my lips over hers then up her cheek bone until I'm whispering in her ear.

"What's your safe word?"

Her breath catches and I smell the fresh wave of slick leak from her cunt and drip on to my cock, the heat of it near scorching.

"Red."

"Hmm." I nibble at her earlobe, tasting the salty skin on my tongue. "Good Omega. Use it if you need it."

She perfumes, a moan slipping from her lips and I pull back, swatting her ass. She yelps but doesn't move, confused as to what I'm asking. My vision darkens and a low growl builds in my chest.

"Run, little Omega."

She blinks and I lean down once more to give my command in her ear. "Run, baby. Or I'll knot you right here on this cold bathroom floor. Wouldn't want to hurt those pretty knees, now would we?"

I spank her ass again—harder this time—and she takes off, my Alpha watching her juicy ass jiggle as we prepare to hunt.

Chapter Sixteen

Iris

I push open the nest doors and run into a hallway. I have no idea where I'm going since I've never been in this house and the most I've seen is the nest and bathroom. I'm faintly aware of a voice calling after me, or voices, but my big-tattooed Alpha told me to run, and I'm not going to deny him. Especially since he's in a rut and I'm going to help him.

Swoon.

The logical side of my brain tells me I should not be swooning at that. I've never seen an Alpha through a rut, let alone during a heat, but rational Iris is not in charge anymore. I'm going by all Omega instincts.

I turn down another short hallway, tits, ass, and stomach jiggling. There's slick running down my thighs and heat licking up my back, the weight of the plug in my ass causing a unique sensation. I hear a roar of my big Alpha who's chasing me in the distance, and I nearly turn back to find him.

"He's in rut!" I hear someone yell, but I keep going.

There's a door at the end of this hallway and I know I'm probably leading myself into a dead end but this is where I'm being pulled too. I push open the dark wooden door, the room decorated in dark browns and burnt oranges. I step further inside and the Prime's scent hits me. It's like walking into a room of crushed mint leaves—bright, sharp, and clean. I close my eyes and inhale long and hard, taking it into my lungs.

This is his room.

I take another step forward, wanting to dive into his bed and make a nest just for us, not caring about being chased anymore. But before I can, the back of my neck prickles and a strong arm bands around my naked waist, tugging me back until the tip of a hard cock pokes me in the lower back. There's something cool mixed in with the heat of it that has me shivering. I thought I felt the same sensation before in the bathroom, but I was too preoccupied with his mouth to look down.

"Gotcha, little Omega."

I half-heartedly struggle, ass wiggling against him so he hisses. It does nothing though, and I don't want it to. I ran for him, he caught me, and now I want him to take me.

"Alpha," I whine.

He chuckles. The sound is deep, dark, and sinful. Like a rich and delicious chocolate mint cake.

"You want me to fuck you hard, baby? Claim this sweet Omega cunt?" His hand slides down to cup my sex, using enough force that I lift up on to my tippy-toes.

"Yes, Alpha!" I cry.

He bends down and nips at my shoulder, not enough to bite through the skin but enough to make me gush slick all over his hand.

"How about that sweet ass that's being stretched out for me. Can I fuck you there, Omega?" He fingers me with his hand on my pussy and uses the other to press against the base of the plug, driving it further in.

"Yes!"

"Remember..." He nips once more at my shoulder before he sucks on it hard. I thrust into his hand, wanting more of his fingers inside me, but he doesn't give in. "Your safe word is red."

"Yes, Alpha!" I cry out, a cramp lancing through my belly.

"Get on the bed and present, Omega."

His bark isn't harsh, but it zips through my being like I've been hit by lightning. He releases me from his grasp and my inner walls clamp down on nothing, my clit throbbing to the point I want to cry.

I scramble on the bed and do what he commanded. Knees apart, ass up, shoulders down, arms flat, and hands crossed in front of me with my forehead resting on the mattress. I'm totally exposed in this position, showing my submission and my need for my Prime. The most dominant and strongest of them all.

Anticipation builds in my stomach, pussy pulsing lewdly. With the view he has, I know he can see it.

"Beautiful," he states. Like it's a fact, not an observation.

I preen, nipples tightening against the sheets. The mattress dips and rough hands drag up the backs of my thighs. He groans and I perfume for him to show him how much I like it, arching my ass back further still.

The warm touch leaves and is quickly replaced by the sting of two spanks, one to each cheek. I cry out against the bed, more from shock than pain.

"You like that, Omega?"

"Yes, Alpha."

A finger dips inside my pussy but leaves as quickly as it came. "I can see that. So wet." I hear a sucking noise followed by a moan. "So sweet."

Hmmm, he tasted me and he likes it. I shake my ass, the action earning me another two spanks, this time a bit harder. The plug inside me shifts in both a pleasurable yet uncomfortable way.

"I'm gonna fuck you now, Omega. Make you feel so good, have you creaming on my cock before I fuck this peach of an ass and knot it full."

His dirty words would have me melting into the mattress if I wasn't already doing so. There's movement next to me before I hear his command. "Look at me, Omega."

I turn my head to meet his gaze. There's light coming in from outside the window covered in sheer curtains. It's not enough to hurt my eyes but enough I can see his harsh masculine features. He's holding his dick in his hand and stroking it.

"The others are nearby if I go too far. Say your safe word or call for them if you need to, understand?" His words grit out, like he's in pain saying it.

"I trust you, Alpha."

His eyes soften and he looks down at his cock. My gaze falls to it and I see why he's saying what he's saying. Not only because as soon as he's knot deep inside me he'll lose himself fully to rut for who knows how long, but because he's massive. And not just that, he's pierced. A silver bar passes vertically through the head of his cock with a few more horizontally on the bottom.

I keen and arch my ass so my muscles strain, unable to say words. I sense the fear of my rational brain, scared of what that will feel like, but I'm an Omega. I'm built to take my Alpha, and I'm not afraid of him or his decorated cock.

"Rut me, Alpha."

Those are the magic words. His eyes that were already dark and dilated churn with carnal need. He moves with lightning speed, taking his place behind me. He drags the broad head of his cock through my wetness, teasing my clit with the cool metal. I whine and moan. Thankfully he doesn't tease me for long. He lines up with my entrance and thrusts inside, pierced cock, inflating knot, and all.

"Oh fuck!"

"Yes, Omega," he groans, one large hand on my hip to keep me steady while he rests the other between my shoulder blades. "This cunt is so fucking good."

He pulls his hips back, piercings dragging against my inner walls, until to my surprise his knot pops out. It stings yet it feels so good; I want him to do it again.

And the big Alpha does, over and over, until I feel it inflate enough. I know if he pushes it back in I'll lock down and he'll come. I want it, want his cum to fill me up, but at the same time I want what he promised.

"You'll get it, Omega," he says.

Right, said that out loud. But good, I want him to know what I want.

I squeeze my pussy around him and he growls, slapping my hip. "Trying to make me come?"

I shake my head. "Need more. Harder."

His hips piston forward, swollen knot bumping against my opening but not sinking in this time. I protest and before I know what's happening he's lifting me up, one arm binding around my breasts to hold me against his chest and his other hand sliding to find my clit.

He thrusts upward in a new angle. I moan wildly from all the sensations in this position. The weight of the plug in my ass is greater here, and his piercings rub my G-spot, his strong fingers circling my clit.

"Your greedy cunt is trying to milk me dry, Omega. You want my cum while you come all over my cock?"

"Yes, Alpha." He thrusts roughly. "Oh, gods!"

He circles my clit faster, the arm around my chest pulling me tighter to him so he can suck my scent gland.

"Gonna bite you right here one day, Omega. Make you mine."

"Do it."

The big Alpha growls. "Don't tempt me."

"Please!"

His teeth nip at the most vulnerable part of my neck, and he bites down, but not hard enough to break skin.

My hips buck and he holds me to him. Rutting into my pussy and using my body within an inch of my life, my arms flopping uselessly at my sides. I love it.

Wilder releases my neck and growls, "Come, Omega. Scream for me."

And I do.

I scream and wail, pleasure sparking through my body like a thousand volts of electricity. Slick and my own cum spill out of me with the strength of my orgasm, my inner muscles gripping his cock tight.

Wilder continues to thrust, hips slapping against mine, the sound indecent and perfect. When he comes he roars, chest vibrating against my back as his seed fills me up and heats me from the inside. Without his knot to lock it in, it spills out of my pussy and down my thighs. I lament at the loss of it and my big Alpha chuckles breathlessly.

He pushes me forward on the bed, his cock slipping from me. I don't like that it's gone but there's no time to think of it because he's rolling me over and commanding me to open my lips.

I do as he says, my gaze locked with his. He holds out his tattooed fingers, the digits covered with his release and mine. "You don't want to waste my cum, Omega, then we won't. Now clean me up."

My tongue darts out, the flavor of mint and strawberry delicious. I moan, grabbing his wrist and making sure I get it all, tasting the salt of his skin along with it. It's so very good and I want more.

I don't have to ask for it, because my Alpha knows. Even in rut he's taking care of me like a good Alpha. Not that I expected any less. He continues the process until his cock is hard again and I'm begging for what he promised.

"You want my fat knot in your ass, Omega?"

"Yes, Alpha. *Please*, give it to me."

"Want your pussy filled while I do?"

My interest piques and fresh slick coats my thighs. The big Alpha laughs lowly, the sound so wicked and yummy I perfume.

"Can our Beta join us?" he asks.

Surprise works up my spine but I'm not going to question his offer. If the Prime wants to share me during his rut, I'm not going to say no. I adore the Beta. I adore all the males in this house. But I miss him and his calm basil scent.

"I'll take that sweet slick and perfume as yes?"

I nod and he kisses me hard on the lips, no doubt tasting us together. When he pulls back we're both breathless and his eyes have darkened again.

"Then let's get him in here."

Chapter Seventeen

August

I've lost track of how long I've been listening to Iris and Wilder fuck. My poor dick is hard and straining, pre-cum staining the fresh set of boxers I put on.

I'm suffering alone out here, but it's by choice. Mateo and Jett went downstairs at least twenty minutes ago, unable to be so close to their pack lead in rut. I could tell it hurt them to walk away, but it would have been worse if they stayed. Especially since they've both been close to falling into rut themselves, being near has them at risk of doing the same.

I've heard stories of more than one Alpha succumbing to it at the same time, and I know Iris is an Omega and built to take them, but she shouldn't have to deal with that. So, my mate and Jett are off getting a late lunch and fixing Iris and Wilder something for when the rut subsides. And I'm on watch duty. We all trust Wilder, of course we do, but this is an unusual circumstance. I told them I'd stay in case Iris needed me to intervene.

Moreover, I'm the best person for the job. I've helped Wilder through a rut before, and I know how he is. I can take his dominance and punishing strength. And while we may not be intimate in the way Mateo and I are on a daily basis, we both love each other. I also have eyes and my Prime is a very attractive Alpha. It's not like I didn't enjoy helping him when he needed me, and he knows I'll always be there for him. He trusts me and I trust him.

"Augie!"

I'm standing up from my spot on the wall in a flash, heart racing by the command in Wilder's voice and the surprise of it coursing through my system.

"Get in here. Our Omega needs you."

I'm walking into his bedroom before I even have time to take a breath. The door had been cracked open, but the moment I'm inside their combined scents hit me like a freight train.

Strawberry, mint, sex—like a mojito on the beach in the summertime. I hold back a groan, dick tenting my underwear.

"He's been waiting to help you, Omega. Look how excited he is."

My gaze meets Wilder's briefly. He's sitting on the bed next to Iris, his hazel eyes black, and thick pierced cock impressive and leaking. He's definitely in rut, but way more coherent than he was the time I helped him. In the hours that we fucked, he'd hardly let up. Grunting and swearing. He wasn't making full sentences like this, or acting like the cocky Wilder I know he can be when he's not in pack leader or business mode. I won't complain about it, because I'm glad he's let me join and his Alpha wants to share. But that doesn't mean I'm not going to be cautious. The last thing we need is to add some Alpha rage to the mix.

"You're here," Iris says from the bed. Or should I say our Omega.

She's stunning. Her generous body is covered in marks from our fingers and mouths, not to mention cum, slick, and sweat. Her face is flushed with desire and lips swollen from kisses. Her legs are slightly spread, her pussy plump and ready to be fucked again.

I cautiously step forward toward the bed, making sure to be aware of Wilder. "I'm here, sweet girl."

She reaches for me, spreading her legs wider to invite me between them. I've had dreams like this before, ones I never even told Mateo about. Visions of us together tangled in sheets while

I made her come again and again. Not only us alone but with Mateo and our pack. I still can't believe this is all real. That my dream girl is here. That she's our mate. Our Omega.

It makes me wish I would have met her sooner. That I'd gone to one of her conventions for *Knot Hollows* or tried to get our pack to hire her for a movie before now. But what's done is done, and that's the past. I'm living in the present, and hopefully after her heat is over she'll choose to stay with us forever.

I take another step forward but when I reach the edge of the bed Wilder stops me. Iris whines, the low keen an arrow to my gut. I swallow and meet my pack leader's gaze. He's half-smiling, stroking his hand down our Omega's arm.

"I'm knotting her ass, and you're going to knot her pussy. Do you understand?"

My heart bangs in my chest and all I can hear is the sound of blood pumping in my ears. There's only two ways I can "knot" an Omega as Beta. One, is if I put on a silicone knot, or two, I use my fist.

I don't have a silicone knot right now so that leaves the latter. I'd imagined doing that to Iris when I was fingering her on the couch, and I'm not going to lie and say I'm not very interested in the idea. And by the smell of Iris's perfume filling the air and fresh slick dripping from her slit, she wants what Wilder is offering. Even if she may not know exactly what that is.

She'll soon find out.

"I understand, Alpha."

Wilder's half-grin turns to a smile that shoots a shiver of anticipation through me that goes right to my dick. He turns to Iris and leans over to capture her lips in his. He kissed her on set, but watching them now in the privacy of his bedroom is erotic to say the least.

Wilder's tattooed hands grip her face, nearly swallowing it whole. Her mouth opens to him obediently and the sounds they make are obscene. I palm my cock through my briefs for some relief, but not enough that I'll come in my pants again.

I'm going to save it all for our Omega. She'll no doubt want it before our time here is through. She drank me down before like I was the best tasting Beta on the planet, and I won't deny that I liked watching her swallow my cum. I want to see her do it again and again.

Wilder pulls back from Iris's mouth. She pouts and tries to get him back but he says something to her I can't hear. He shifts her toward the edge of his bed and places a pillow under her hips and head. When he's satisfied, he kisses down her neck and over her breasts. His strong hands palm them, squeezing them hard so she cries out. When he's done playing, he makes his way over her stomach, kissing each line and mark, before kissing down to her pussy.

I squeeze my cock harder and pull air into my lungs the moment Iris cries out. She grips his dark hair beneath her fingers as he swirls his tongue around her clit, lapping up her slick until more drips out and he does the process again. It doesn't take long before she's writhing on the bed and begging.

"Alpha, please. Aug—" She reaches out for me as an orgasm hits her with a brutal force. Wilder takes the moment she arches off the bed in pleasure from his tongue to remove the silver plug from her ass. The action elicits a high keening noise, and Wilder uses one of his hands to motion me to them while he helps our Omega ride through her orgasm with his mouth.

I cautiously move on to the bed, the mattress dipping under my weight. Wilder looks up at me, mouth and beard soaked with slick. I tap into our bond and am hit with not only his pure and pressing arousal, but gratitude toward me being there with him. It's odd considering the situation, but now I'm curious if ruts with scent-matched Omega's are different from normal ruts. Another thing to Google when I'm not getting ready to dive fist first into our Omega's tight pussy.

I smirk at Wilder and he mirrors the same expression back, as if he knows exactly what I was thinking about. He glances down to my hand then to Iris. "Go slow."

There's no bark in his command but I'm not going to disobey his request. I replace Wilder's mouth with my fingers, lazily playing with her over-sensitive clit. She tries to arch into my hand but Wilder pins her legs open.

"Stay still, Omega," he demands. "Our Beta is going to make your pussy feel so good before I knot your tight little asshole."

Fuck. I forgot how dirty Wilder can talk. It's hot to say the least.

I shift on the bed so I can use both hands. I continue to circle her clit slowly while I collect slick with the other. When it's nice and wet, I make eye contact with Iris.

"If it's too much, tell me to stop."

She nods vigorously, eyes glossy with pleasure and lost to her heat. I'm not sure she knows exactly what I'm going to do but she'll figure it out soon enough. I dip two fingers inside her, ignoring whatever Wilder is doing for now. He'll make it known if he wants me to stop or do something different.

Iris's pussy grips my fingers, already greedy for more. I wet my lips and slide my fingers further in until I'm knuckle deep, curling them and dragging them over the spot where a knot would usually lock.

"Yes!" she cries, her body trembling with her need. "More! I need more!"

"I know you do, sweet girl. And I'm going to give it to you."

I add a third finger, then a fourth, moving in slow circles before pushing them in and out, the squelching sounds sexy as hell.

"She's ready," Wilder says. His tone is a near growl that alerts me he's hanging on to himself by a thread again. No doubt the need to knot his Omega and ease her discomfort riding him hard, even more so since he's in rut.

"I'm going to knot you now, Omega."

She blinks at me in surprise and I return it with a playful smile, forming my hand into a duck bill. My entire hand slips past her opening, her pussy sucking me in. She cries out and I place my free hand on her lower belly to sooth her.

"Look at you," I say in awe. "Taking my knot like such a good Omega should," I tease, forming my hand into a fist inside her so she feels what I'm saying.

She gasps, hips lifting. "Oh my gods!"

"Not a god, Omega. Your Beta." I travel my hand up further, to the place where a knot would go and slide my other hand to her clit at the same time. She detonates on my fist, muscles clamping down as if it's a real knot.

"That's it, Omega. Come on my knot."

She writhes and shakes, the sensation of her body milking my fist nearly making me come again from no contact. Omega's bodies during a heat are a thing of beauty, and I'm so lucky Iris gave our pack the privilege to be with her now. To do something like this and have her so openly give us everything she has. I don't think I'll ever get over it, and I can only hope they'll be many more heats like this and I'll get to do this again with Mateo. I know he'll love it.

There's a nudge at my shoulder and I glance up at Wilder. Pure lust covers his face, the muscles in his neck strained as he jacks his angry-looking Alpha cock up and down, pre-cum leaving from the slit and his knot beginning to swell.

"Keep still until I tell you to move."

"Yes, Alpha," I reply.

I don't miss the way Wilder's cock jerks in his hand, my submission turning him on. I smirk a little but turn my head away so he doesn't see it. Just because we're not intimate with each other normally, doesn't mean I don't like that I can arouse him.

"You ready for my knot in your ass, Omega?" he asks Iris.

Her pussy clenches around my hand in response before her verbal yes follows. He knee walks up the mattress and I move out of the way as best I can. The position we're in is a unique one, but doable. Thankfully I don't mind having an up close and personal experience of Wilder knotting our Omega's ass for the first time.

He pushes up Iris's leg, bending it in a frog-like position. The pillow under her hips gives him better access to her back entrance. He gathers the slick from her multiple orgasms and coats his cock with it then dips two fingers inside her ass. Iris moans from the pleasure and I use my free hand to hold her as still as possible while flexing my other one inside her.

"Alpha," she begs. "I need you."

Wilder doesn't make a smart remark or answer her with dirty words. His rut is taking over now and once again I'm honored that he's let me join in.

He presses the head of his pierced cock against her tight ring of muscle. The tip slips in and Iris moans, muscles fluttering around my fist. Wilder groans as he sinks into her tight entrance. Inch by inch of his shaft along with the silver bars disappears as he goes, his thick cock stretching her hole obscenely around him.

I fucking love it. It's one of the hottest things I've ever witnessed, and by the way Iris screams in pleasure and grips my fist, I know she loves it too.

Wilder bottoms out, his swollen knot bumping against her asshole.

"Fuck her with me," he growls. "I want her to come on my cock before I knot her."

"Yes!" Iris whines. "Feels so good. So full. Need more."

Wilder laughs darkly. "Greedy, little Omega."

Our Alpha nearly pulls all the way out before thrusting back in, taking care not to be as rough as he would be if I wasn't forearm deep inside her. I feel him moving, and I swear I even feel the piercing through the head of his dick dragging back and forth against the barrier between us. My cock jerks again, reminding me that it's there and wants attention.

I pull my hand back after Wilder thrusts back in and I lean forward to lick her clit. Iris bucks, and I plunge back in, opening and closing my fist a few times until I'm rubbing on the spot that makes her quiver.

"You gonna come, Omega?" Wilder grunts, rutting into her faster now that she's warmed up, his hand gripping her outer thigh in a hold that leaves indentations on her skin.

"Yes!" she cries.

"Do it. I want to feel you choke our knots, baby," he demands.

Iris wails, her body jerking and inner walls trying to lock on to my fist as another orgasm pulses through her body. Her eyes that she'd squeezed shut fly open, just in time for me to see them widen as Wilder thrusts forward, his knot popping into her tight ass.

Her pussy gets impossibly tighter on my fist from the stretch of Wilder's cock and growing knot. It's a sensation I won't soon forget, and Iris's eyes roll back into her head as Wilder's knot swells to its largest point.

"Gonna fill you up, Omega. Make you mine," he groans.

"Alpha!" she cries, voice husky and nearly gone from all her screams. "Yes!"

"Perfect Omega," he grunts as he comes, hot cum spilling inside her and heating my hand. "You take your pack so well. Just like you were meant to."

Wilder's words wrap around my heart and squeeze. My gaze falls to Iris, her skin wet and flush, eyes hooded with satisfaction. He's right about everything he said. She's perfect, and she's meant to be ours. Every moment she spends with us only proves it further to me. There's no way in hell I'd be in this room during Wilder's rut in the position I'm in if she wasn't.

Wilder fucks his knot inside her slowly, tugging it back and forth and nearly making Iris come again, but our Omega is rung out.

When he's given everything he can to her, and the aftershocks of her orgasm have faded, I slowly pull out, memorizing the image. Iris is already asleep by the time Wilder's knot has subsided enough that he can slowly shift them on to their sides, tucking her into his chest before his eyes find mine.

The hazel of them is back, meaning his rut is fading. It's shorter than I expected, but add that to another weird thing about Iris and the last twenty-four hours. I'm grateful, because now we can bring her back to the nest and attend to the rest of her heat as a pack. I slowly start to get up off the bed when Wilder stops me.

"You can stay with us."

I shake my head and glance down at my tented boxers then back to him. "You rest then get Iris back to the nest. I'm going to find Mateo, he's been feeling everything through the bond. He needs me." And I need him.

Wilder smiles back lazily, his eyes already drooping. Even without the chaos leading up to this moment, our Prime is exhausted. He's been carrying too much for too long, and having to delay the movie because of Iris's unexpected heat probably didn't help. The Alpha needs rest, and the comfort of his Omega. Come to think of it, that might be why his control finally slipped and he went into a rut.

I'm nearly at the door when I hear Wilder say, "Thank you, Augie."

I turn back, our bond buzzing with gratitude and contentedness. Something I don't think I've felt, at least not this potent, in a long time.

And that's all because of Iris Walker.

"No thanks needed, Alpha."

Chapter Eighteen

Iris

"Let go, Iris. You're safe with us. Your Omega can fully take over now."

"You like the taste of our cum all together, don't you, mi conejita?"

"Yes, sweet girl. Suck just like that."

"Your hot cunt is squeezing my knot, baby."

"Such a greedy little Omega, wanting us to fill all your holes."

"Doesn't your Beta look good eating your pussy with Mateo's cock in his ass, Omega?"

"Rest now. We'll be here when you wake up, star."

My eyes fly open and I sit up straight in bed. The movement is way too fast and a wave of dizziness washes over me like cold water being dumped on my head. I shut my eyes and groan.

"Easy now, Iris. You're okay. Take a deep breath," a warm voice requests, a hint of a twang beneath it. I do as he says, Jett's lemon scent washing over me as I inhale deeply through my nose.

His purr springs to life before he continues. "That's it, and now out...yes, good girl."

My overused pussy clenches at the praise and I grit my teeth. *No. No more of that.*

"Can you open your eyes for me?"

There's part of me that doesn't want to. Doesn't want to face the reality of what's happened with Pack Quinn for the last...gods knows how many days. But I know I have to. What other choice is there?

I press the heels of my hands to my eyes, trying not to think of everything that has to happen now that I'm out of my heat. I take another few breaths before I finally feel collected enough to face the Alpha. We're alone in the nest, lights twinkling above us. I'm wearing a baggy shirt they must have put on me, one that smells of mint.

My body naturally relaxes, as if it's now been programmed to be eased by the Prime Alpha's scent.

"You okay?"

That's a loaded question, one I'm not going into right now or ever. So I nod and turn to look at Jett. He's watching me carefully, a blanket tugged up over his waist, leaving his chest bared to me. If there was a window in here, I have no doubt that if it's daytime, the sun would be shining on him like a perfect halo, highlighting his flawlessly askew sandy hair and muscled chest.

I've looked at Jett plenty in photos and movies over the years, but seeing him now, after days of fucking, he's something else. He appears lighter, relaxed, and without the haze of heat I can fully appreciate his toned frame and the tattoos inked across his skin. My eyes zero in on one cascading from the top of his shoulder and spilling onto his left pec. It's an intricate ocean wave in black and grey, the details of it so good it appears real—like it will roll off his skin and lap at your feet. Visions of my tongue tracing it before I kissed down his body enter my mind and I can't stop the flush that now burns my cheeks.

"Do you like the ocean?" he asks.

My eyes meet his and I find no cocky grin or knowing look on his features. Bless him for not bringing up what I was just thinking about, even though it's written all over my face and my scent has spiked. You'd think after a heat that wouldn't be a problem, but apparently not.

"I do."

Jett smiles. "Ever surfed?"

I shake my head. "I have crap balance."

"Maybe you just need the right teacher. We could go sometime if you'd like."

The apples of his cheeks stain red and my heart speeds up. Did Jett Quinn just say he could teach me to surf and blushed? Does he forget I ruined his movie and fucked things up royally for their pack. For me?

The bridge of my nose stings and my scent goes sour at the same time Jett's lemon does.

"It's okay if you don't. It's not for everyone."

"No, I—" My throat is thick with emotion and I swallow it down, deciding it's best to change the subject before I have a breakdown. It wouldn't be hard with the after-heat hormones coursing through my body. It's also been a long time since I came down from a heat with a pack, and they're my scent matches. If I could describe how I feel right now, I'd simply go with wrecked. Wrecked in so many ways.

"Iris—"

I can't take the worried tone in Jett's voice or the way his brow knits in almost fear. The muscles in his arm twitch as if he's going to reach out to touch me, and I need to get out of this bed before that happens. I don't want to accept anymore from them. I'm surprised he's even being this nice to me now.

"Can I use your bathroom to clean up?" I cut him off, already shifting off the bed. My Omega protests, not wanting to leave our warm, safe nest that smells like Jett, Mateo, Augie, and Wilder—like pack.

Unfortunately, this is not our pack, and it's not our nest.

It is. They said we're theirs.

I gently remind the fragile demon inside me that it was all heat talk. Nothing they said was true. It hurts to think of it that way, but it's how these things work. The last time I was at a heat clinic the Alpha's would say the same kinds of things.

It wasn't the same.

"Of course you can," Jett says. "You don't have to ask."

I don't bother looking at him, pushing slowly off the bed, ignoring the delicious aches in my body as I move.

"Do you need help?"

A memory of him washing me during my heat appears in my mind. He was so tender, so caring. I didn't have to beg for him to knot me, he knew what I needed and said sweet things to me while he used some sort of buzzing waterproof toy on my clit.

My soured scent starts to turn sweet and I shake my head. "It's okay. I'm good."

His eyes burn into the back of my head as I walk away, the T-shirt hardly covering my ass. I'm about to open the bathroom door when Jett's voice rings out behind me.

"Iris!"

I turn and he's standing at the end of the hallway with tight briefs hugging his lower half. Damn this man. He has to look like an underwear model right now? I'm sure I look like I've been put into the washer and set on spin.

He walks up and holds out his hand. "I thought you might want your phone so you can check in with Sadie and anyone else who may be missing you."

Tears prick my eyes before I can stop them. Gods. I need to shower and get these hormones under control. I can't cry every time they do something thoughtful. I've already proven how out of control I am by going into heat on set. If I have even a small chance at keeping the role, which I doubt I do, crying and acting weird is not going to help.

I take the phone from his hand, careful not to touch him, muttering a "Thanks," before I escape into the safety of the bathroom, and locking the door shut behind me.

"Six days?"

"Y-yes," Sadie squeaks through the phone.

"That's—that should be impossible. My heats are usually four days tops."

"It's because of the suppressants and touch starvation. I'm sure meeting your scent-matched pack also has something to do with it."

I run my hand through my wet hair as I sit on the edge of a massive jacuzzi tub. One that could easily fit three big Alphas, a curvy Omega, and a toned Beta.

I shake the thought away and focus on the facts at hand. I was fucked for six days straight. I remember the first two of them including Wilder's rut, the rest are coming back to me but they feel like broken bits of hazy dreams.

Gods. That means the film has been delayed for longer given I remember my heat breaking sometime yesterday morning, Augie mentioning it was breakfast time, and Mateo coaxing me to drink a smoothie before I fell into a deep sleep. It's morning again now, and the date on my phone confirms it's been seven days since they brought me here.

"Iris?" Sadie questions.

I blow out a breath. "I guess that's true. I'll have to make an appointment with my doctor to make sure everything is alright. Not the fancy one that fucked me over but my normal one."

"Already done. It's in your calendar."

"Thanks, Sadie."

"But you're alright otherwise? They took care of you?"

My chest warms at her concern. I remember how she stood up for me before everything went down too. Ready to pull me away from Pack Quinn if I hadn't consented to them helping me through my heat. She's a good person and friend.

"Yeah, they did."

"Then why do you sound so stressed?"

I stand from the tub and pace back and forth, biting my nail. "Because I fucked up, Sadie. I went into heat on set, ruined the movie and my career, and made this pack take care of me for a week!"

"Did they tell you that?" she asks angrily. In my head I imagine her standing up with a little snarl on her face, ready to throw down. It has me smiling despite everything.

"No, they didn't."

"What did they say?"

I shake my head even though she can't see it. "Nothing yet. I woke up and came to the bathroom to shower. I haven't faced them yet."

"Then I think you should be talking to them instead of me. Also, how are you even talking to me?"

"What do you mean?"

"Oh, well, when my sisters come out of a heat they spend at least a couple days in their nest resting with their packs. You were going at it for a long time, I'm surprised you're conscious." She snorts, then clears her throat. "Sorry, that was unprofessional."

"It's fine, Sadie. You're right, but it's not my nest and they aren't my pack." Though my Omega did protest to my shower. I was both crying and growling through the entire thing, but it had to be done.

There's a pause before Sadie speaks again. "Aren't they going to be though? They're your scent matches."

"That doesn't mean they want to bite me and keep me forever. Like I said, I ruined everything by being so reckless. I'm sure what happened has slipped to the press. I'll never work again. Especially if they decide to sue me for breach of contract. Which would be in their right since I lied about being on suppressants and—"

"Iris!" Sadie cuts me off. "Calm down, okay? You need to talk to your pack."

I want to reiterate they aren't my pack but instead I pinch the bridge of my nose. "Do you know something I don't?"

"Just talk to them, and we'll speak when you come up for air."

"Sadie—" The line goes dead and I pull my phone from my ear to see she did, in fact, hang up on me.

I stalk over to the mirror, any relaxation and relief I'd felt from finally having a proper heat gone from my body. I stare at my reflection, anxiety written clear as day all over my face. If I go out to talk to Pack Quinn like this, their instincts will be to comfort me and I'll probably end up letting them. But we need to have a real conversation. Not one clouded by our designations or the intimacy we shared together over the last freaking week.

"You really had to go all out, didn't you?" I ask my Omega.

She ignores me. Of course she does. Though I swear I feel pride toward her actions flitter through me.

I puff out a breath. I need to find clothes that aren't Wilder's shirt and put on my acting face. I'm going to find the pack and apologize for what happened. I just hope I can walk away with my dignity and the possibility of a career.

Chapter Nineteen

Iris

JETT WAS GONE FROM the nest when I finally came out of the bathroom, and in his place were my clothes laid out with a note.

Augie washed these for you. Come downstairs for food when you're ready. —Jett

Not only did they take care of me during my heat for six full days plus an extra day of sleep, but they washed my clothes and now they want to feed me? There was even a new pair of underwear folded in the pile in my correct size. What the hell?

It's because they're our mates. They're kind.

Yeah, yeah. My Omega is very pleased with them and I would be too if they were my pack. But I'm still convinced this is about to go south, and I'm not going to pretend like when we talk this is all going to end up like a fairytale. Real life isn't that way. I learned a long time ago that everything comes with work and time put in. That's how I even got as far as I did in Hollywood. Sure, the scent match part feels magical, but the rest of the story is not.

I reach the end of the hallway and find a staircase. Now that I'm no longer in heat, I can appreciate the home. I have no idea what part of Los Angeles we're in, but the house is large and modern in the style that reminds me of the Hollywood Hills. Despite the openness and sleek lines, it feels homey, decorated with modern paintings on the walls. Looking closer at one, it looks like a graffiti artist did them with broad lines of sprayed paint in all different colors and shapes.

When I reach the bottom of the steps, I hear voices and smell bacon, eggs, and something sweet cooking, along with the notes of mint, lemon, honey, and the undertone of basil. My mouth waters and my feet carry me toward the scents, my stomach growling and my Omega perking up.

I warn her that this isn't going to turn into some post-heat fuckfest which makes my strawberry scent sour. I roll my shoulders back to get control of her and keep my feet moving toward the masculine voices that become louder with each step.

A large kitchen comes into view as I turn the corner, and in the back the sunshine of morning fills the space with natural light. Wilder is standing with his broad back to me, washing his hands at a sink while the other pack members sit at a dining table in front of him. They don't notice me as I approach, their conversation continuing.

"I don't think keeping her on is a good idea," Mateo says.

Jett sighs. "Yeah, I will say the chemistry was a bit off to begin with," Jett says. "And things have changed now."

"Augie?" Wilder asks.

The Beta pushes his glasses up his nose. "I have to agree, things have changed. I don't think it's a good idea to go with her now."

Wilder shuts off the water and leans on the sink. "I agree. She's a great actor, but Iris is—

A whine bursts from my throat before I can stop it. Four sets of eyes snap in my direction and I debate between running away or curling into a ball on the floor right here and dying.

I told you. I told you. I told you, I chant to my Omega. I should have just left and cut my losses. Had my lawyer and agent be my point of contact with them from here on out.

"Iris." Augie darts up from the table and heads my way.

I hold my hands up to keep him at a distance. "No, it's okay. Don't comfort me. I'll call a ride and go." The words feel sticky on my tongue and my stomach bubbles at the idea of leaving. Which is ridiculous since they just said they're going to replace me. That Jett doesn't have chemistry with me.

There's a chorus of growls, the loudest coming from Wilder. I know because it's deep and powerful, the same kind of growl I heard while he chased me in his rut.

"Go?" Augie looks genuinely confused. "We made a big breakfast."

The sadness in his voice is laughable. I want to question it, tell him how ridiculous it is that I heard them all speaking of me like I'm yesterday's news and then offering me food, but I don't want to cry.

"It's best I leave."

The Alpha's approach, Mateo next to Augie, and Wilder and Jett on his other side. It reminds me of when we met on set, their pack standing in a semi-circle looking at me. It feels like yesterday, even though it was a week ago now.

"We don't want you to go," Mateo says.

"You should get some food in your stomach and then we can talk," Wilder adds.

I can't hold in the half laugh, half sob that comes out of me. "You want me to do all that after I just heard you talk about replacing me?" I look at Jett. "After you said we don't have chemistry?" My voice nearly breaks on the question, and Jett has the audacity to look like I just ripped his heart out.

"No, Iris. We weren't—"

I hold up my hand to cut Jett off. "It's okay. I get it. I shouldn't be upset. You all were gracious enough to help me through my heat, a heat that never should have happened in the first place."

"Iris—" Wilder tries to interject but I shake my head.

"It's fine, really. I mean, it's not fine. I was reckless coming on set when I did, and I put not only all of you at risk but your crew."

"How were you reckless? You met your scent-matched pack. These things happen," Mateo says.

I blink at him. "These things don't just happen."

"Not often but you couldn't have predicted this. It wasn't your fault," he adds, the sincerity in his voice killing me.

"But it was," I retort.

"Iris—"

"No, it is. I tried to tell you and Augie in the car but my heat took over. I wasn't on suppressants anymore when I saw you all that first day. My new doctor wouldn't fill my prescription like he said he would."

A low growl builds in Wilder's chest. "And why wouldn't he?"

My eyes move to his. He looks scary, like he's about ready to strangle someone. I want to say he's mad at me but my Omega isn't afraid of him.

"Because I've been on them for a year."

Tension clouds thick around us like humidity in the summer. The scent of the males in front of me turning acrid. Mateo swears under his breath and Augie rubs his back, his own features pinched.

"A year?" Wilder repeats.

I nod. "Like I said. This was all my fault. This job meant a lot to me and I fucked it up. Not only my career and my reputation but I ruined your movie and probably pissed off your investors. We'll be lucky if it's not leaked to the tabloids by a crew member. Or I should say, I'll be lucky. They won't eat your pack alive like they will me."

"Iris—" Jett tries but I can't let them attempt to make me feel better.

"Really, you guys are better off finding someone else who won't screw things up. I'll be okay, at least I hope. So like I said,

I should go. You don't have any responsibility to me now. You all did your duty to an Omega in need."

Pack Quinn stares back at me, their scents still tinged with anger and something else. If I was listening to my gut I'd say pain, but that would be ridiculous.

You're being ridiculous.

I want to growl at my Omega but I don't. I know she's grown attached to this pack.

You have, too.

I haven't, have I? I grip my fists at my sides.

There's no way I'm attached to them. I can't be. Six days of wild and hot sex does not equal a lifetime relationship. I remember telling them not to bite me, and like the good pack they are, they honored my wishes even when my Omega begged. But at the end of the day, I'm not part of their pack, and now they don't want me on their film. Which is understandable.

I ring my hands in front of me and avoid their eyes. "Okay, then. I'll see you around."

I'll see you around? Why the hell would I say that? I really do need to get out of here.

No, please, my Omega whines, the sound almost escaping from my throat. *They're mine.*

It takes all my strength to move my body in an effort to turn around and leave. I'm almost looking away from them when Wilder's voice curls around me like a hand on the nape of my neck, firm and unyielding.

"Where do you think you're going, Omega?"

There's no bark in his question, but the cool and possessive way he says it reminds me of how he was in his rut. The way his arm banded around my chest when he caught me and everything that followed.

My scent goes from sour to welcoming, the sweet scent rising around me. I clear my throat and attempt to focus, putting as much dominance as I can find into my own eyes before I look into Wilder's strong gaze.

"I told you."

"You didn't say where you were going."

I huff. "If I need to be specific, to my nest."

"Your nest is upstairs."

My heart stops in my chest and damn it to hell, my nipples pull tight. The reaction brings forth a memory of Wilder talking about piercing them while Jett fucked me. I'd never thought about it before, and now I have a feeling I'm going to think about it every time I look at them.

My cheeks warm and I force myself to stand firm. "That's not my nest."

"It isn't? I clearly remember you calling it yours."

"I didn't mean it. I was in heat."

He steps closer, and when I stupidly don't retreat, he takes another one, our bodies close enough I smell his minty scent and feel the delightful power of his Alpha. I'm only a day out from the end of my cycle, and if I didn't know any better, my body feels like it might be gearing up to go again. Which is absolutely not going to happen.

Wilder cocks his head to the side, eyes softening. "I don't want to believe that to be true, Iris."

His answer surprises me. I thought he would have said something cocky back, trying to make me believe that I did. But there's a sadness in his tone that both confuses me and makes my Omega want to comfort him.

"Is it only because I'm your scent match?" I swallow hard to keep from crying.

Mateo steps forward so I can see him again, neck slightly tilted in submission to show me he's not a threat. "It's your nest because you're ours, mi conejita. The scent match is a beautiful bonus, but we want you for you."

"That's impossible, we just met."

Augie clears his throat and joins Mateo. His features flushed and eyes bashful. He pushes his glasses up the bridge of his nose, the action reminding me of the other times he did that over the last week.

"We may have just met, Iris, but I think this pack feels like they've known you for a long time."

My brows furrow. "What do you mean?"

He rubs the back of his neck. "I planned to tell you how much of a fan I was of your work before everything happened. To be honest, I've had an embarrassingly large crush on you for a long time. My pack can confirm."

"Large is even an understatement, mi amor. Sometimes I feel jealous."

They share a lover's smile, and Mateo presses a kiss to his mate's knuckles before they both turn their gaze on me. The warmth between them shifts, wrapping around me too. Butterflies stir in my stomach, and my Omega preens under their attention.

"You're being serious?" I ask.

Augie's confirming nod only intensifies the flutter of wings in my belly. "I know it's not the same as knowing the real you, Iris, but you're everything I've dreamed and more. I think my instincts knew who you were, even through a screen. I've felt a pull to you from the moment I saw you. Don't you feel it?"

His question echoes the one he asked me on set, before I agreed to come here and let this pack to see me through my heat. He presses a hand to his chest and I mirror his action. Just like before, there's a pull there. One I felt the second our eyes connected on set, and my Omega trusts him implicitly. She wants me to run and jump into his arms right now. Let his calming energy and earthy basil scent soothe us.

I nod before I can think better of it, which makes his smile widen.

"There's something else." He looks over to Jett before he continues. "We figured something out while you were asleep. Tell her."

Jett steps up to complete the semi-circle again, but this time there's hardly any space between me and the pack. My eyes connect with his ocean blue ones, and that tug Augie made me aware of only grows stronger.

"Were you at the Producer's Guild Halloween party in Beverly Hills two years ago?"

I raise a brow in question, but I nod.

Several emotions cross Jett's face, but his shoulders relax before his lip tips up in a smile. "We were, too."

"I don't remember seeing you there."

"Because we were there all but thirty minutes before I went into a rut and we had to leave."

"That was you?"

Jett rubs the back of his neck. "It was. I don't remember scenting you, but my Alpha must have known you were there. He wanted to find you and we couldn't."

Ours. They're ours.

I want to tell my Omega otherwise, but I know she's right. I've known their ours, but—

"I hear what you're saying, but I told you what I did. And you all were just talking about replacing me." I stare directly at Jett. "You said we didn't have chemistry," I repeat.

"We weren't talking about you, star," Jett insists, distress laced in his tone that upsets my Omega.

"Then who?"

"We were talking about a film we're changing the production schedule of, one that came after *Knotting Hill,*" Wilder says. "The Omega actor playing the opposite of Jett was already cast."

My face falls and jealousy rears its ugly head out of nowhere. My Omega growls, the sound low and menacing, one I've never made before—at least while coherent.

I force it down and press my lips together in shocked embarrassment. I expect the males in front of me to react negatively to it, but instead the four of them grin at me like that was the best thing they've ever heard.

"That's why we were discussing her part," Mateo says. "Because none of us feel comfortable with Jett starring opposite an unbonded Omega."

"Especially so soon after we've found ours," Wilder says.

My gaze meets his and for a time, I don't know what to say.

"You really all feel that way?"

"Without question," Augie says.

"But I ruined everything!"

"You ruined nothing," Wilder declares, tone final. "I'd argue the opposite."

"He's right, Iris. You made everything better," Jett says.

I huff out a disbelieving laugh. "You're just trying to make me feel better."

"Omega," Wilder barks.

My eyes snap to his simmering ones, his gaze zeroed in on me.

"I want you to listen to me." He holds out his hand and when I don't stop him, he cups the side of my neck, thumb holding the curve of my cheek.

"I'll only say this once, and I mean every word. You're not only our mate, but you're smart, talented, and perfect. Our pack nearly ruined everything because our idiot asses didn't push to hire you when we should have. Had we gone with our guts instead of our investors you would have been ours sooner."

"But—"

"May I finish?" He doesn't say it in annoyance, but with a wily grin tugging at the corners of his bowed lips.

"Yes, Alpha."

His eyes darken and his hand on me flexes.

"You shouldn't have lied about the suppressants, and my Alpha is upset you were on them for so long and we weren't there to help you before now, but on our pre-production call, you told me this job meant a lot to you and why, so I understand why you did what you did, especially if your prescription was denied."

I'd forgotten I spilled my guts to him about the role in *Knotting Hill* being my dream, and what it could do for me. But I do remember hanging up and wondering why I'd felt so comfortable with him, and even thinking his voice reminded me of a soothing cup of peppermint tea.

I inhale, leaning into his hand and scent marking it. Wilder's minty pheromones intensify as he rubs his thumb on my cheek, the adoration and awe in his eyes evident.

"I'm sorry," I exhale.

"You have nothing to be sorry for. The crew won't say anything, they're good people and are under NDAs like all of us are."

I breathe a sigh of relief. "But the movie?" I look at the rest of the pack but they're all smiling.

Wilder directs my gaze back to his. "The pack is funding the rest of *Knotting Hill*, and production is set to continue in two weeks if that works for your schedule."

Excitement blooms in my chest. "Really?"

"Yes, really. The movie wouldn't be the movie without you, star," Jett says.

"Wait. Why two weeks?"

Wilder drops his hand and steps back so I can take in every pack member before he declares, "We were hoping to claim our Omega."

There are moments in life where you know you're going to remember them forever. When you feel the earth move beneath your feet, and the DNA and elements that make up your body transform, and your memory burns the experience so deep into your being, no passage of time will scrub it away.

My first day on the *Knot Hollows* set, getting the call from my agent with the offer to play Juliette, and meeting Pack Quinn—my scent matches—were three of those moments.

And now...

Three Alphas and a Beta who only met me a week ago, who took care of me at my most vulnerable, who very much want me and need me like I need them—even if I've been trying to deny it—want to claim me as their Omega.

What is life right now?

Ours. Bite. Please!

Perfume bursts out of me in a cloud of strawberry haze. Slick dampens my underwear and leaks down my thighs. Wilder's nostrils flare, taking in my scent before releasing a groan. I'm aware of Jett, Mateo, and Augie doing the same, purrs springing to life in the Alphas' chests along with their pheromones, Augie's basil almost as strong.

"Yes." My single word hangs in the air, the pack's eyes all on me unblinking as if they can't comprehend that I said yes.

I close the distance Wilder created, my gaze locked to his. "Bite me, Alpha. Make me your Omega." I look into the rest of the pack's eyes. "All of yours."

When I meet Wilder's hazel gaze again, his purr dominates over the other's, the veins of his tattooed neck flexing. He runs his tongue along his canines and looks down at me with heat, the intensity of him flooding my greedy pussy with more slick.

I allow my instincts to take over, to show him that despite my earlier fears, I'm theirs for the taking. My Omega has been telling me from the start that we belong together, and I'm not going to fight it anymore. I trusted them enough to fully surrender to my heat, to let them take care of me when we didn't even know each other. I even trusted Wilder in a rut—and now...

I'm going to trust myself. It's high time that I do. I got this far in life relying on myself, and now I can do it alongside an amazing Pack. We can figure out everything else later. But I want them—no, need them—*now*.

"I want this." I show my throat to Wilder. "If you'll still have me."

The Prime is silent as he reaches for me, his fingers stroking down the side of my neck, over the bruise he left during his rut. The "fake claiming" mark to satisfy my Omega. I shiver at the sensation, another wave of arousal heating my core and saturating the kitchen with my scent.

"There will never be a point in time where we don't want you, Iris Walker."

The rest of the pack chimes their agreement and my eyes water, this time not with tears of distress, but happiness.

"Now"—he kisses me once—"we'll take you up to your nest"—another kiss, rougher—"and I'll sink my teeth into this perfect throat"—a third kiss, hungrier—"and then your pack will claim you—fuck you hard, fill you so full—that you'll never forget who you belong to."

I clutch his arms, my nails biting into his biceps, and repeat the word we all need to hear. "Yes."

Chapter Twenty

Wilder

Iris clings to me as I rest her on the nest mattress, the sheets smelling of pack and lust. I lay over her body, trapping her beneath me, my cock hard against her belly.

"You're wearing too many clothes, little Omega," I groan.

She nips at my lips and I kiss down her throat, anticipation of what's to come thrumming through my veins.

"Then remove them, Alpha."

Her sassy comment makes me chuckle against her scent gland, and I both hear and feel the amusement of the rest of my pack through the bond. They're all on the mattress with us now, ready and waiting for me to claim our Omega. The gift we thought we'd never get but have been blessed with all the same.

"Are you a brat, Iris?" She thrusts her hips upward, seeking more friction in answer.

"What do you think?"

I take her lips in mine, sucking on her tongue, exploring and tasting her before kissing downward again, starting to open the buttons of her shirt, revealing inch by inch of her soft skin I spent the last week worshiping.

"I think you're a sweet Omega, who wants to be good for her Alpha."

She teasingly bites her lower lip. "My Omega maybe, but me? Not so much."

"Is that so?"

Her eyes shine playfully as she grinds her pelvis up against my hard cock so I hiss. I bend my head forward and bite her nipple through the fabric of her bra. She cries out and clutches my hair, pulling at its roots, holding me to her breast as fresh slick dampens her already soaked jeans.

Fuck. She's perfect. Not that I didn't already know that.

Iris's marathon six-day heat was unexpected, glorious, and chaotic. Between her touch starvation, my rut, and the fact I now know she was coming off a year of suppressants, her cycle was a whirlwind of need and desire. Iris's Omega was soft, sweet, and demanding, but overall pliable and submissive.

Now I get to learn everything about Iris, who's apparently a brat. My pack and I are going to have so much fun exploring this facet of her. But not right now.

I rip open the offensive bra covering her heavy tits, taking her nipple directly in my mouth and sucking.

"Fuck! Oh, Wilder."

My name on her lips is like a jolt to my already hard cock and I know the time for waiting is over. I move down her body, taking off her clothes as fast as I possibly can before removing mine.

Her curved form is covered in marks from days of fucking, but it's missing the most important one. I kiss and suck over bruises and surface bite marks, over her belly and breasts until my lips are sealed with hers again.

Our tongues stroke and fuck, her slick-soaked slit dragging over the throbbing shaft of my cock. I break the kiss and lock her silver eyes with mine, lining up my pierced head with her entrance.

"Are you ready to be mine, Omega?"

Her fingernails drag down my back and she thrusts her hips up in answer, my cock slipping inside her pussy.

"Claim me, Alpha."

"Don't you dare look away."

I sheath myself inside her in one rough thrust, her eyes flying open and her mouth forming a silent scream as she stretches to fit me.

"That's it, Iris. You feel how you were made to take me?"

She nods, keeping her eyes open while I fuck into her fluttering cunt. "Feels so good, Alpha. Don't stop."

I press my forehead to hers and piston my hips, my knot swelling. "Going to knot you now, baby. Fill you and claim you. Tell me again how much you want to be mine."

"I want to be yours, Alpha. I want to be part of your pack. Please, I need it. Need you. Bite me!"

I roll us on to our sides with my back facing the rest of our pack and her eyes to them. I want her to see them when I claim her officially as ours. She wraps her leg over my hip and pulls me closer, licking my scent gland before baring her throat.

I drop my hands to her ass, and grip, thrusting up hard and fast, my knot locking into place. Iris cries out and comes hard, choking my knot and triggering my orgasm. I come violently, holding her trembling body, and zero in on the spot I marked during my rut.

"Do it!" she cries.

My vision goes white and I lunge forward, sinking my teeth into her throat. The copper tang of blood and the salt of her skin floods my mouth, a tingling sensation filling my chest as our fresh bond begins to form.

I pull slightly away and grip the back of Iris's head. Her body trembles with her pleasure but I gently guide her to my throat. "Bite me, baby. Make me yours."

Her teeth bite into my flesh without hesitation and my knot grows larger; I come again without warning, Iris following into another release. Her pussy clenches down hard on my knot and it takes a moment, but when her orgasm subsides she gasps. After we've both cleaned our new marks on each other, our watery eyes meet and I brush a tear from her cheek.

"I feel you," she says.

Her new bond in my chest is still solidifying, but I feel it. Feel her. Her awe, her joy, her arousal. Her sweet and soft Omega along with her strong and determined edges. Like I already knew, Iris Walker is perfect.

"I feel you too, Omega."

Iris peeks over my shoulder at the rest of our pack, her body still trembling with the aftershocks of her pleasure and newly formed bond.

I brush my hand down her hair and will her body to release me. I'd love nothing more than to stay knotted with her all night, but she needs the other's marks on her body, I can feel how much through our bond.

I bring her attention back to me. "Are you ready for more?"

The release of my knot and the thrill of excitement she sends through our bond is all the answer I need. I press my lips to her ear and give her a command, "Present for your pack, Omega."

Chapter Twenty-One

Mateo

An Omega presenting is the ultimate form of submission, and there was no pause in Iris's movement as she did what Wilder requested.

He trails a hand down her back, praising her for a job well done. From the vantage point I have near the lower part of the bed, I get an obscene view of her pussy, slick and Wilder's cum leaking from her still fluttering hole and dripping down her thighs.

"Mierda." I run my hand over my face. My cock aches and my teeth are no better. Watching Wilder claim our Omega, feeling the new faint connection of her through my pack bond, I'm wound tight. My Alpha wants to plunge into her warmth, put his teeth into her shoulder, feel the bond form completely and know she's ours.

"Mateo," Augie snaps me out of my trance. He grips my hand and brings it to my lips. "She wants us to bite her together."

Iris's head is turned to us, eyes glimmering with need and hope. I flip my mate's palm over and kiss it. Feeling his happiness pour through our bond. A Beta doesn't need to bond a pack Omega if the head Alpha has marked her and she him, but the fact she wants to do it only proves how right she is for us.

"You want that, mi conejita?"

She nods, wiggling her plump ass. It reminds me that while she was preoccupied with Wilder's rut, I ordered a butt plug with a tail attached. Augie's genius idea, and I can't wait to use it on her one day. A day that will happen soon now that she's chosen us.

"Then we will give it to you," I promise her.

Wilder sits back on the mattress next to Jett to give us space, the blond Alpha of our pack patiently waiting. I'd invite him to join us, but after seeing him with our Omega in her heat, and the emotions in his bond, I know he wants to do it alone.

He acknowledges me like he knows what I'm thinking before I give my full attention to the two most important people in my life. Mi amor y mi Omega.

Augie's already undressed, his cock ready with pre-cum gathering at the tip. He and Iris watch as I remove my clothes, my knot beginning to form. There were moments during her heat where her Omega requested I fuck Augie while he fucked her or ate her out, but now she gets to experience us together and without the haze of heat.

"On the bed, mi amor."

Augie quickly lies next to Iris, and I move so I'm on her other side. I swipe my fingers through her slick and Wilder's cum, dragging it up until I shove it back inside her. I pump two fingers in and out, and she moans for me, pushing back on to my fingers wanting more.

"Suck your Beta's cock, Iris. I want to see you work him up before we both fuck your pussy."

I don't think either register the last part of what I said, and if Augie did, he can't say anything because his eyes are rolling back in his head as Iris shifts her position and takes the head of his cock in her mouth.

His hands grip the mattress and Iris moans, both from the taste of him and my fingers working her pussy. She's so wet and ready that it doesn't take long for me to feel comfortable for what we're about to do.

I remove my fingers and place my hands on Iris's waist. She pops off Augie's cock with a small protest that makes all of us sans Augie chuckle.

"Don't worry, greedy girl. I'm going to help you sit on his cock, then I'm going to knot you, and we're going to bite you together."

She looks over her shoulder at me. "Both of you in…"

"Your tight pussy?" I finish for her with a smile. "Yes." I lean over and lick her slit, tasting her from the source before pulling away again and gently smacking her ass. "You can take us."

Augie holds his cock and I move Iris, helping her sink down on his long length. She moans, head falling back and my own dick twitches at the sight of her hole swallowing my mate up inch by inch.

I wait until she's adjusted before I move between Augie's spread legs while she grinds her clit on his pubic bone and starts to beg for more, her Omega becoming restless for more bonds.

Our Beta mate holds her hips. "Lean forward, sweet girl. We're gonna bite you, don't worry."

Iris comes to him, meeting his lips in a delicate kiss as their chests press together. I pump my cock, gathering some of the slick leaking out from Iris's pussy and off Augie's already soaked balls for lube. They whimper into each other's mouths at the contact and my knot aches at how sexy and sweet they are together.

I press the tip of my cock into Iris's already stretched opening. She cries out and I press my hand on her lower back. "Breathe, mi conejita. We're going to make you feel so good. Aren't we, mi amor?"

"We are," he says, kissing her softly. "We're going to take such good care of you."

Iris relaxes at our promise, and my cock sinks in, gliding next to Augie's in the most sinful friction. I keep pushing forward, one of my hands gripping her hip and the other moving up to press between her shoulder blades until my cock is completely seated and my knot bumps against her opening and Augie's balls.

"You both feel so good." I let out multiple curses, getting myself under control so I don't come until my knot is lodged inside her.

It takes a minute for her to adjust, but when she does, she nods at Augie to give him permission to move. He thrusts up and when he pulls back I move in. Her perfume is everywhere in the room, telling us how much she likes what we're doing. We lunge in and out, my cock working against Augie's while Iris's pussy grips around us in fluttering beats.

"Mateo!" she screams. "Gods please! Augie," she begs, her teeth nipping at his pec, almost breaking the skin.

I take her hair in my hand and pull her back. "No bites yet, Omega."

"Please, I'm gonna come. I need it!"

"Mateo," Augie grits as she squeezes our cocks. "It's time, baby."

I lock my eyes with my mate and I give him a firm nod. I draw back almost all the way and thrust in, my knot forcing itself into Iris's body with Augie's cock.

"Fuck!" she keens. "It's so much, it's—"

"Just breathe, sweet girl. We've got you," Augie chants, the bastard thrusting up as much as he can against me. His movement along with the heat and suction of Iris's pussy does me in. My knot expands, and I lock inside her, keeping Augie with me so he can no longer move. The sensations are intense, and I come. Harder than I ever have in my life.

"Now," Wilder's gruff voice barks.

Iris jerks between us as my teeth sink into her back shoulder and Augie bites near her collarbone. Her taste floods my mouth and my cock jerks, the warmth of my mates' release and the forging of Iris's bond inside my chest too much but not enough.

I'm about to tell Iris she needs to bite me when she lifts up between us and asks for my hand. I give it to her willingly and she sinks her teeth right between my thumb and forefinger. Sparks shoot up my spine and more of my cum jets out, filling her up as our bond completes. Her beautiful soul taking space beside my mate's.

It isn't until the fog of my orgasm clears that I see she bit Augie too, right where she'd been playing before on his pec. Satisfaction fills my chest, my heart growing if that's even possible. I meet Augie's gaze as Iris rests between us, a smile on her face and joy in her dilated silver eyes.

"Te amo," he mouths to me.

I mouth it back, knowing that one day soon we'll be saying it to the woman between us. I know we love her already, I can feel it flickering in the bond. But for now, I enjoy the moment and the beginning of something new and beautiful.

Chapter Twenty-Two

Jett

I KISS UP IRIS's legs, taking time to worship every inch of her. During her heat, she needed us, needed to be rutted and knotted. Her Omega demanding to be filled and bred until she passed out and started the cycle over again.

She was beautiful and soft, pliant beneath all of us, and pleading. This Iris, the one not clouded by heat, is equally as stunning, but I like that she's here and fully present. That her eyes are clear and I can enjoy this moment, one I'll only get this once.

The bites my pack gave her has increased her sex drive, and her perfume is like a drug. My cock is hard and ready. I suck and bite her slick inner thigh, her hands are gripping the tips of my hair to try and pull me up. I hum a laugh and continue to play, not giving in. She whines, annoyed, but I explore every curve and inch of her, tracing my tongue over the perfect imperfections of her skin. The intoxicating smell of her pussy has me delirious, but I ignore the pang of my knot and drag my teeth over her quivering muscles.

"Jett," she moans and wriggles. "Touch me now, I need it."

I look up at her from between her legs. "Touch you where, star?"

"You know where. I don't want to beg." She parts her legs further in invitation, slick and the cum of my packmates making her messy. I do what Mateo had done before me, and start to push their seed back in.

She sighs at the feel of my fingers inside her, and I insert them further. There's a squelching sound that makes her full body blush, but I don't stop. I use my other hand to play with her overly sensitive clit and she tries to close her legs.

"Don't, Iris. Keep them open."

She drops them back open and I move my fingers faster, curling them so I stroke her G-spot. Her toes curl and her back arches off the bed. Faster and faster I go, her strawberry scent becoming thicker and stronger as she approaches her orgasm. The next time we do this I'm going to handcuff her to my bed and use a vibrator on her clit, but my fingers will do for now.

"Jett!" Her inner muscles tense. "Jett! Fuck, Jett!" She sounds panicked and I pretend not to know why. I stroke her harder yet, and when I know her release is about to happen, I gently pinch her clit.

Her cum soaks my fingers and down my wrist, dripping onto the bed. I would take time to enjoy the fruit of my labor any other day, but my cock is hard and ready, knot swollen and needy just like her pussy.

I slip my fingers from her, and with lightning speed flip her over onto her belly. I slide home in one long thrust, knot and all. My hips slap against her ass and she screams in pleasure, hand flying back to grip my backside.

"Oh, Jett!" she moans, arching her butt back to take me deeper.

"You're so wet, Iris. So full of your packs cum, aren't you?"

"Yes, so full. I love it."

My heart flips and I pull back so my knot almost comes all the way out before I thrust back in. "You want my cum, star? My bite?" I push her hair aside and lick at the nape of her neck.

She shivers, squeezing her pussy around my cock in an attempt to catch my knot.

"Do it, Jett. I need it. All of it. Make me yours."

I place my forearm to where she can reach it, and with one last rough thrust my knot locks into place. "You're already mine, Iris Walker."

I come with a growl, my teeth biting into her flesh. She does what I hoped and bites into my forearm, right over a cluster of star tattoos. It's everything I could have dreamed of and more.

I lick at her bite to help it heal and she does the same to mine, feeling the strength and joy of her bond actualize in my chest. Like the north star to guide me home.

When our orgasms subside, I turn us to our sides and kiss her neck. She releases my knot and Wilder, Mateo, and Augie move into a cocoon around her. Wilder at her front, Augie and Mateo finding a space between her legs and near her head.

Our scents all twine together and the warmth of Iris buzzes through our pack bond, making it complete. No one speaks, but no words are needed. We're all together, Iris is ours, and Pack Quinn is better for it.

Epilogue
IRIS

ONE YEAR + ONE WEEK LATER

"Iris, over here!"

"Look here, Iris."

"This way, Iris!"

"Omega!"

Wilder growls and points at the photographer who just used his bark on me and my designation, telling security to throw him out. I step and repeat until I reach him, his arm automatically tightening around my waist. The rest of our pack is on the other side of him, smiling for the cameras.

"You didn't have to throw him out," I say through my teeth, keeping a well-practiced smile on my face.

"Of course I did." He smirks down at me. Wilder always looks bad-boy handsome, but even more so tonight for the premiere of *Knotting Hill*. He's wearing a casual black suit and black shirt, his hair is gelled back at the top, beard freshly trimmed, and my healed bite mark on his neck proudly on display amongst his tattoos.

The matching bite on mine tingles just thinking about that day a year ago when Pack Quinn claimed me, and I claimed them. We had a bonding ceremony on a private beach last week on the one-year anniversary. It wasn't anything overly fancy that would draw attention, only close friends and family were invited, but it was beautiful and ours.

And tonight, we're finally showing the world Augie's masterpiece. We've seen the film already, even snuck into test screenings around the city to see peoples' reactions, and so far it's been a hit. There's early Oscar buzz for Jett and my performance, and every press outlet is calling us the new "it" Hollywood couple, both on screen and off.

Good thing we've already got our next film in the works. This one Augie and Mateo wrote together, something they'd been secretly working on for a few years. When they told us all about it, Wilder and Jett were shocked to say the least. Apparently they had no idea Mateo had any interest in writing. It didn't shock me, however. Mateo is a creative person just like the rest of his pack. He's also Augie's mate. It made sense to me with the amount of time they've spent together over the years that they would work on a project together in a larger capacity.

The story is a moving one, about an Alpha and Omega who meet in college, but life keeps pulling them apart and reuniting them at the worst possible times. I have no doubt that next year they'll both be winning awards for how beautiful and poignant it is.

Wilder squeezes my waist and I stare up at him. He smiles, adoration shining in his hazel eyes as he tucks a strand of curled hair behind my ear before leaning down to kiss my forehead. I melt into it, drawing in his love and strength. The cameras flash like crazy but I ignore them.

Jett, Mateo, and Augie approach us, dressed in similar suits to our Prime but in varying colors. They all circle around, touching me in some way as they close in for pack photographs. Mateo's hand secretly grabs my butt and I try not to laugh when

I turn to kiss his cheek then blow a kiss to my blond Alpha and sweet Beta.

More cameras flash and my pack gathers in closer, Mateo and Wilder making me laugh when they start to whisper flirty and dirty things in my ear. The photographers love the joy radiating off us, and so do I.

If you had asked me a year ago if I'd be walking down the red carpet for *Knotting Hill* with not only a career soaring to heights I've always dreamed about, but a pack that loves me wholly and completely, I would have laughed in your face. I thought that I couldn't have one without the other, but Pack Quinn has proven me wrong.

Was building a pack hard? Yes. It continues to be some days. We all have our ups and downs, and we worked backwards with how a modern-day pack would usually come together. But we made it work. They courted me, took me on dates, integrated me into their studio, and I got to know each of them for who they are beyond what they show the world.

Wilder is fierce and loyal, tough and scary on the outside, but soft on the inside. He's silly and romantic when he's alone with me and our pack. We love to go on motorcycle rides down the coast and go for ice cream dates. I always laugh with him and my Omega is at ease when he's around.

Jett is my light in the darkness, someone I go to when I need to reconnect with myself and nature. If I'm his star, then he's my compass. He's taught me how to surf—though I'm not very good—and we love going star gazing together on the beach and finding all the best burger places in town when we're not filming.

Mateo can be similar to Wilder in some ways, which is why they often push each other's buttons. But unlike our Prime, he doesn't give one persona to the outside, he just is who he is. He's devoted to his pack, his family, and especially Augie. We can spend hours in bed talking about anything, and he loves to take me on spontaneous adventures and snap far too many photos of me when he finds good light.

Last but not least, there's my Augie. Creative and kind, the dictionary definition of a Golden Retriever mate. He's my deeply sensitive and kind soul who writes me poetry and knows enough film and TV trivia to keep me entertained for hours. Don't tell my Alpha's, but he's the best cuddler. If I ever need a hug, I go to him first.

"Iris," Mateo says softly in my ear, pulling me from my thoughts. "They're calling everyone in to watch the movie."

"Sounds good." I take a step forward but Wilder and Mateo's grip on me tightens. I look up at them then over to a smiling Jett and Augie. No, not smiling, smirking.

Every one of my packmates is smirking, the mischievous nature of it making butterflies erupt in my stomach and heat course through my body. If I wasn't wearing the special Omega panties that Wilder got me that conceal the smell of slick, there's no doubt even the photographers would be scenting strawberries right now.

Mateo's lips brush the shell of my ear and I shiver. "We're not going to see the film, mi conejita."

I swallow. "We're not?"

"Nope," he says, popping the P.

I don't have a chance to ask where we're going, because I'm ushered off the red carpet toward the entrance to the theater. I spot Sadie as we approach, who's become like a little sister to my packmates. She's speaking to another Beta assistant, a flush on her cheeks. When she spots me her cheeks get redder and I make a note to ask her who that is later.

"Are you all ready to go in?" she asks.

"We just came to tell you we're taking Iris on a little adventure," Jett says, Mateo's hand on my back guiding me past her. When her wide eyes meet mine briefly, the only thing I can do is shrug because I have no idea what's going on.

"What?" she sputters. "But the screening!" Her worried voice follows us.

"We've seen the film already," Wilder notes.

"But the after party!"

"We'll be there," Jett assures.

More butterflies build in my stomach from the anticipation of whatever is going to happen, as I'm guided through the theater doors, my silver body con dress made of shimmering material catching light as we step through the doors.

"Are you going to tell me where we're going?" I ask, Jett and Augie now in front of us, Mateo's hand still on my low back and Wilder's between my shoulder blades.

"Have patience, sweet girl," my Beta says playfully over his shoulder.

I puff out a breath as I'm led past the front of the lobby of the theater where people are mingling, some I know and some I don't. My pack waves and greets those who try to stop us with promises of seeing them soon and to enjoy the film. An announcer over a speaker calls everyone into the screening so they can start the movie on time, but that's the last I hear before I'm led to an entrance behind the theater that says employees only.

Jett holds the door open for us and I grip Mateo's arm as I walk up a flight of steps. When we reach the small room at the top, I know immediately where we are.

"The projection room?"

Once we're standing near the center of the space, Mateo pulls me back against him so my ass is pressed to his groin. I gasp when I feel his half-hard cock. His fingers hold my hips and he shifts my hair to the side to run his nose along my scent gland.

"We thought since we've seen the movie, we'd watch it from a new perspective."

He pulls me back tighter and grinds his hips into me, replacing his nose with his tongue, licking over my rapidly beating pulse.

My hand flies back to coil in his hair, and I raise my gaze to meet the rest of my pack who have gathered in front of me. I'm aware the film is starting because the projector comes to life—everything is remotely run these days—and the already dim room gets darker due to the light in the theater going down.

"We're not watching though, are we?" I say quietly, my question ending on a gasp as Mateo sucks on my neck with more gusto.

Augie steps forward and shakes his head, his finger tilting my chin up. He leans in so his lips hover over mine at the same time Mateo nips my neck.

I gasp and Augie captures the sound with his mouth, sealing his lips over mine in a heated kiss. By the time he pulls back I'm breathless and my underwear are ruined, the scent of strawberry filling the air alongside my pack's heady cocktail of honey, lemon, mint, and basil.

"No, we're not," he teases my lips. "But we are going to fulfill the next fantasy on your list."

I pull back just enough to see his eyes that are glazed with need. When Pack Quinn started courting me, we made a list of things we all liked and didn't like in the bedroom. Mine included a list of kinks and fantasies I've always had. We've worked through most of them, the most recent one was Mateo's favorite. Augie and Jett helped me find the sluttiest bunny costume available. That sounds funny when you say it, but I got custom ears and a butt plug that had a grey poof on the end. I'd already had one Mateo got for me, but this one matched the ears and vibrated.

I rode him and he made me come again and again and again, but not before he and Jett edged me for at least an hour straight with toys while Wilder gave them directions on how to make me squirm and Augie watched like the good boy he is until Mateo allowed him to come inside my ass.

The thought of that night makes my pierced nipples harden around the silver barbells Wilder picked—the piercings themselves a gift I got for him to further mark our bond. I bite my tongue to keep from moaning and the scent of my perfume overtakes the small room.

"You wanna be fucked in public, sweet girl?" Augie asks, his voice roughened by desire.

My first reaction is to say yes. I've been wanting to do something like this with them for awhile now, and while technically Augie and Mateo eased me on set during my heat last year, the set had been cleared. There was no chance of getting caught and there was definitely not an audience in a theater just beyond a wall.

Speaking of...

"Won't they hear us?" I ask, eyes flicking behind him.

"Soundproof," Wilder replies. "But I wouldn't be too loud, little Omega."

My pussy flutters at his endearment and my Omega preens.

"Do you think you can manage that?" He steps closer beside Augie, his presence large and dominating as it always is. "Or we could gag you."

"Oh, she'll be gagged alright," Mateo mutters against my neck, his hands sliding up to palm my aching breasts through my dress. "But with one of our cocks."

My pussy clenches around nothing and I drop my head further to the side so Mateo can get to more skin.

"Please," I whine before I can think about it further.

"Please what, star?" Jett asks, walking around to Augie's other side, my pack now surrounding me. Just how I like it.

In the theater I hear laughter at something that has happened on screen, and I'm sure if I really paid attention I'd hear mine or Jett's voices. But none of that is important. I'm so turned on I think I could be anywhere, even out in the front of the theater with the audience, and I'd drop to my knees and beg for them. The hours I spent in hair and makeup be damned.

"Please, fuck me. Use me."

Wilder growls and Mateo's cock kicks against my ass. Augie leans down to kiss me again and his basil scent envelopes me along with Mateo's honey. I open my mouth to his and groan into it, his tongue twirling against mine and massaging it.

Augie continues to kiss and explore me, his hands dropping to my hips and pulling me forward while Mateo pulls away. He unzips my dress and I note the air doesn't feel cool on my skin that's starting to feel like fire, but I don't care right now. I only care about their touch and getting their cocks in me.

I'm stripped and moved toward the corner of the room. Eventually Augie passes me to Jett who looks so handsome in his blue-grey suit. Another time I'll have to enjoy how he looks, because I want him naked. I want them all naked.

Jett kisses me hard, his lemon taste sweet and tangy on my tongue. I work my hands into his jacket pushing it off. When that's gone, I remove his shirt and drag my hands up his strong chest, following it with kisses until I latch on to his neck and suck, wanting to leave a mark.

"Iris," he groans.

I ignore his call for me and dip my hand into his pants, wrapping my fingers around his hard shaft.

"Need you," I moan.

"Iris," he says again, gripping my cheeks to pull me away. He looks into my eyes, his own swimming with desire for me. "Are you feeling okay?"

"Never better," I say honestly. "Just need you. All of you."

He stares at me another long moment before he finally nods, his lips molding hard to mine before he steps back and Wilder takes over.

Each one of my pack kisses differently. Wilder is the most demanding. His mouth takes mine like it belongs to him, my needy pussy clenching around nothing as his sheer dominance washes over me.

Need to taste him.

I would normally tell my Omega to cool it, but I'm in agreement here. I manage to pull away from his lips and drop to my knees on the carpeted floor. I undo his belt and look up at him, feeling powerful down here despite how tall and impressive my Prime is. He lets me do what I want, pulling down his zipper and taking his cock out.

The ruddy head is swollen and leaking. I lick up the pre-cum, his mint flavor strong and potent. I groan and use my other hand to squeeze more out, the taste of him both satisfying my Omega but also making her—*me*—more ravenous.

"Fuck, Iris," Wilder mutters. I suck him deeper and he threads one hand through my hair.

I make pleased noises around his shaft, sucking and pumping it with my other hand. My pussy throbs and before I know what's happening a whine breaks free from my chest that was probably too loud, even for soundproofing.

Wilder pulls his cock from between my lips and gets down on his knees in front of me. He takes my face like Jett had, eyes searching and nostrils flaring wide.

"Omega," he grits out. "I thought we had another week before your heat was due."

I frown, brows knitting together. "I'm not in heat."

"It's pre-heat. She's having a spike," Augie says from somewhere behind me.

I try to push away the cloud of arousal in my brain but it doesn't take me long to know he's right. I'm so wet I'm leaking down my thighs, and my skin feels as if I'm being burned alive from the inside out. My stomach cramps as if to say, "Yep, he's right" and I would have doubled over had I still not been in Wilder's hold.

"Bring her here. Over on the blankets," Mateo says.

I don't have time to question how they got blankets up here, or the fact that means they planned ahead and got permission to be here, because the need inside me explodes tenfold and I start to beg for them to fill me.

"Shhh, little Omega. Your pack is going to take care of you now," Wilder says, easing me down. Instead of blankets I'm met with the naked warmth of my lemon-scented Alpha. He bands his arms around my waist and holds me to him, his lips against my ear.

"We're gonna fill you so full, star. Make you leak our cum all night. Everyone is going to know what we did and who you belong to. Would you like that?"

"Yes, Alpha."

His rumbling purr vibrates on my back and he brings one of his hands down to play with my pierced nipples. Mateo approaches from the front, naked now and stroking his cock. From this angle he looks especially attractive, like a king looking down on his kingdom.

"You like what you see, amor?"

"Yes, Sir," I cry out when Jett's fingers find my clit.

"Hmm, I like what I see too. Tu cuerpo es exquisito." *Your body is exquisite.* He gets down on the blanket so he's between Jett's legs. Despite all my Alpha's not being intimate together, over our year together and another heat six months ago, nobody is shy doing anything around anyone.

Mateo reaches down and when I hear Jett groan and his purr falter, I know he's getting help from my sweet-as-honey Alpha. Mateo uses his other hand to gather slick from my pussy, then dips his fingers into my ass, stretching me before guiding Jett's wet tip inside the ring of muscle.

Jett holds me tight, sliding one hand to hold me by my throat while the other plays with my clit, lifting his hips to thrust in, stretching me with his fullness.

"So tight, star. So good."

I don't have the capacity to speak so I just nod, my muscles clamping down around him.

"Look at that," Mateo hums. "Gonna fill your pussy now, Omega. Stretch you wide around my Alpha cock."

"Yes! Please, Sir, please! I need you so bad."

Mateo is usually one to take his time, but not right now. It's not what I need. It's not what any of us need.

He gets into position and plunges into my pussy. His cock sliding easily inside me, his and Jett's shafts gliding past each other with only my thin barrier between. The two males curse and I cry out loudly.

"I think our Omega needs her mouth stuffed," Mateo says through gritted teeth.

"I think so, too." Wilder kneels down by my head, turning my face to him. He's naked now too, massive cock hard and leaking with his piercings gleaming. He reaches out and flicks one of the silver barbells through my nipple, smirking when I gasp.

"Open that pretty mouth of yours, Omega."

Before I do I find Augie who's standing guard. He's gotten rid of his clothes, watching us like he loves to do while pumping his cock.

"Augie," I bleat out as Mateo and Jett find a new rhythm. One where Mateo nearly pulls all the way out and thrusts back in so his knot bumps against my opening.

"Yes, sweet girl?"

"Fuck Mateo into me."

Mateo groans and Wilder chuckles.

"Seems our Omega is not so sweet after all," our Prime muses.

"Oh, she's sweet." Augie smirks. "Sweet to me." He blows me a kiss and walks away, rustling around until he comes back with a packet of lube.

We've done this before, so I know Mateo's okay with it. Really okay with it if I go by how his cock feels even larger and hotter inside me, and the way his fingers are gripping my waist tighter.

"If that's what my Omega wants." Mateo stops thrusting to swivel his hips in a circle. "But do it quick, mi amor. She's choking our dicks."

Jett grunts in his agreement and another small cramp hits me. The scent of my arousal and need takes over the room and my Omega rises to the surface.

"Iris." Wilder takes my chin so my attention is on him. Our eyes meet and I know my Prime felt it. He knows what I need.

He dips his thumb between my lips and I open for him, sticking my tongue out. In my peripheral vision Augie works Mateo's ass, getting him ready to take him. Jett thrusts into me from below and before I can scream in pleasure, Wilder stuffs his fat cock into my mouth, pulling my lips wide.

My vision whites for a split second at being filled, the sensations in my body and the scents around me only increasing. Time stills the moment my Beta finally thrusts inside our mate. Mateo stifles a loud groan, swearing under his breath, his cock pushing inside me even deeper from the force of Augie's thrust.

I suck on my big Alpha's dick, his piercing bumping the back of my throat. He's been training me to take him all, including his knot in my mouth. I haven't done it yet, but by the look in his eye I know that's changing right now.

He holds my head between his big palms, guiding my mouth up and down his arousal. I suckle and moan, his minty taste cool, sweet, and salty all at the same time.

"Oh, fuck, mi amor." Mateo has fallen forward so his face is near my breasts. "I forgot how big your Beta cock is."

There's a soft smack that tells me Augie spanked him. He'll pay for that later but I know he'll think it's worth it.

"That's it, baby," Wilder says when I relax my throat. The head of his cock slides down deep and his knot bumps my lips. "Do you think you can take it?"

I hum and nod as best I can. He strokes my cheek and reminds me to blink three times if I need him to stop.

Jett fucks up into me harder and his knot bumps against my already stretched back entrance.

My body tenses at the idea of being so filled outside of a true heat.

"You were made for us, star. Remember that," Jett says. I'd say he read my mind but I know he could feel my trepidation through our bond. "Let us make you feel so good."

He soothes his hands down my sides since Wilder is supporting my head and I relax, my mouth opening wider for my Prime so his knot eases past my lips.

Augie must be sending some of his soothing energy through the bond as well because a calm washes over me that only he can provide. I hum in pleasure and look into Wilder's adoring yet heated gaze as he works his knot the rest of the way in, his cock stuffing my throat full.

Pack. Ours. Loved, my Omega chants senselessly. But she's right on all accounts.

I lose myself to my bonded mates, Jett's knot working into my ass and starting to swell, Augie fucking Mateo into me over and over again so that my breasts jiggle and I swear I can feel his beautiful cock inside me as well as my two Alphas.

The very second Mateo's knot finally pops in, Wilder's knot expands to the point it's almost locked behind my teeth.

Mateo's knot grows too and so does Jett's. My body feels as if it's exploding yet not full enough. It's a strange thing to experience, but I love it, and I need to come. Need them to come.

I express my need through the bond and like the good pack they are, they give it to me. Augie shouts that he's coming and fingers swirl around my clit, another hand pinching my nipples. Mateo moans and his knot locks into place, his cum shooting deep into my womb, the heat of it almost too much to take.

Jett is saying something, I think that he loves me, and his knot pulses with his release, seed emptying in me as he bites into my shoulder. My greedy body takes every drop he and Mateo have to give, yet I need more.

"Inhale through your nose, Omega." Wilder's bark zips through my spine and it's like a bomb going off. His knot locks behind my teeth and I come, shattering into a million pieces. Wilder holds me still, his cum filling my mouth. I swallow his lust for me and continue to orgasm, my body shaking with so much pleasure I start to cry.

All my Alpha's purrs fill the room to comfort me and Wilder wipes away the wetness from my cheeks, releasing me when his knot starts to subside. I take in a breath and he kisses me, not caring I taste like him and I'm probably a mess.

"You did so well, Iris. So good and perfect for us. Our Omega."

I purr in pleasure and happiness, letting my pack take care of me. They speak more words of praise and love as I fall into sleep.

I wake up a short time later to the sound of clapping and cheers, my face pressed into Augie's pec right where my healed bite mark is, and Jett's broad chest behind me with Wilder playing with my hair and Mateo massaging my calves.

"Welcome back to the land of the living, star." Jett kisses my shoulder right over Mateo's claiming mark and I blink sleep from my eyes.

"You hear all that clapping?" Augie asks when I focus on his sparking gaze.

My skin flushes as everything we did back here while an audience watched our film floods back into my mind.

"I do," I say.

"It's all for you," Jett mutters.

My body heats and I shake my head, sitting up to go into my Prime's arms, leaning back against his chest so I can see all our pack.

"No, it's for us. For our pack. We did it."

Wilder kisses the top of my head, while Jett, Augie, and Mateo look on with happy smiles on their faces.

"That we did, Omega. And we're gonna do it again soon," Wilder teases, clearly not talking about a movie.

My pack snickers and I smack his arm playfully. "Not here."

"That's right. We have a party to attend."

"And a nest to build," Jett adds.

Right. I had a heat spike, which means my heat is on the way. I pry myself away from my pack, knowing I have to get away from them if I don't want to spike again. Once we're all dressed and Augie tells me they have hair and makeup waiting for me to freshen me up, I walk to the door ahead of them, stopping to look over my shoulder.

They all stare at me for holding us up and I put on the sweetest smile I can possibly muster, deciding now's a good time to tell them I also had a surprise planned for tonight.

"Did I mention I went off birth control for this next heat?"

"What?" Wilder balks.

"Yep. You'll have to draw straws over who knocks me up first."

Excitement, surprise, and arousal all woosh down the bond at me like a massive ocean wave. We've been talking about children more in the last few months, and while I didn't think I'd want them so soon after our bonding, I know with my pack I can have it all. Motherhood, a career, *everything*.

Mateo and Jett growl with need and my pussy clenches. Wilder lunges for me but I run out of the room before he can grab me, giggling all the way down the stairs. Later, when my heat starts, we can work on making babies. For now, it's time we celebrate our pack's success, and have a glass of champagne while I can.

Acknowledgments

My first omegaverse is complete! This was so incredibly fun to write, and I loved every second of it. I hope you did, too! I've been wanting to write one for years now since I'm an avid omegaverse reader, and now that I finally have, I'm ready to write more!

Now on to the thanks!

Massive thanks to Esther Reid! You've been my omegaverse expert during this. Thank you for reading it multiple times, for listening to my voice notes, and for helping make this the best book possible. I couldn't have done this without you.

I've got to thank my dear friend and fellow author Rebecca Kinkade for not only beta reading but helping me sensitivity read for Mateo and helping me make sure the Spanish was correct. Shoutout to Ambar Cordova for triple checking my Spanish as well. You both are incredibly amazing and thank you for supporting me.

Thank you to my beta readers, Blair F, Randi, Becca G, Sarah U, and Allyson M. It was so fun to see your feedback and commentary on my first ever omegaverse! I can't forget Jono for helping me come up with the title for Lights, Camera, Knot, and for listening to me talk about knots for months on end.

This wouldn't be a Kayla acknowledgments section without thanking Nic Reeves. Thanks for being my rock and for formatting another one of my books! Can't forget to thank Brenna Jones for another amazing cover and the incredible artist

Fremuard who brought the Quinn Pack to life! And of course my besties, Bailey Hannah and Elliott Rose. As always, thanks for being there for me and helping me with this book when I needed it.

Lastly, I always want to shout out my Smut Obsessed and Smut VIP members over on my Patreon: Meghan K, Alonja W, Athena, Riotgirl915, Stephanie, Tiffany S, Sarah U, Nicole A, AlyseMarie W, Candice L. C, Joy S, Gertie, Caitlyn L, Katelyn W, Michelle C, MoonViolet33, Natalie D.R., Danielle P, Blair N, Roksy, Holly D, Necia M, Jessica M, Lindsey M, and Carlee R.

Till next time...
Xoxo,
Kayla

Also By Kay Lynn

Want More Pack Quinn?
Get Their Bonus Chapter:
https://www.patreon.com/posts/151026940

Pre-order Book 2: Knead, Want, Knot
https://www.amazon.com/dp/B0GNX3XBB1

Love Kay Lynn's heat?
Turn up the temperature with her
spicy contemporary romances
published under Kayla Grosse:
http://www.kaylagrosse.com

For Exclusive Bonus Stories, Artwork, and More Visit:
http://www.patreon.com/kaylagrosse

Find Kay Lynn:
Website: http://www.kaylagrosse.com
Instagram: @kaylynnauthor
Facebook: Kaylaholics Facebook Group
TikTok: @authorkaylynn

About the Author

Kay Lynn is a pen name of Kayla Grosse.

Kayla Grosse, author of the international best-seller Trick Shot: A Spicy Christmas Novella and a collection of sweet and spicy plus-size romances, grew up in a suburb of Madison, Wisconsin. Though she lived near a big college town, her backyard was a cornfield, and her favorite hobby was riding her horse and imagining herself

flying through the fields with a cape on her back and a sword in her hand. Her overactive imagination led to writing lots of FanFiction, scripts, and publishing several books. When not writing, Kayla can often be found riding horses or drinking fancy espresso. She lives in Los Angeles, CA with her cockatiel, Fiyero, and Quarter Horse, Atlas.